MARY LOUISE IN THE COUNTRY

EDITH VAN DYNE

1st WORLD
LIBRARY
Literary Society

Mary Louise in the Country

Edith Van Dyne

© 1st World Library, 2009
PO Box 2211
Fairfield, IA 52556
www.1stworldlibrary.com
First Edition

LCCN: 2009923375

Softcover ISBN: 978-1-4218-8824-8
Hardcover ISBN: 978-1-4218-8923-8
eBook ISBN: 978-1-4218-8725-8

Purchase *"Mary Louise in the Country"*
as a traditional bound book at:
www.1stWorldLibrary.com/purchase.asp?ISBN=978-1-4218-8824-8

1st World Library is a literary, educational organization
dedicated to:

- Creating a free internet library of downloadable ebooks

- Hosting writing competitions and offering book publishing
scholarships.

Interested in more 1st World Library books? contact:
literacy@1stworldlibrary.com
Check us out at: www.1stworldlibrary.com

1St World Library Literary Society

Giving Back to the World

"If you want to work on the core problem, it's early school literacy."

- James Barksdale, former CEO of Netscape

"No skill is more crucial to the future of a child, or to a democratic and prosperous society, than literacy."

- Los Angeles Times

"Literacy... means far more than learning how to read and write... The aim is to transmit... knowledge and promote social participation."

- UNESCO

"Literacy is not a luxury, it is a right and a responsibility. If our world is to meet the challenges of the twenty-first century we must harness the energy and creativity of all our citizens."

- President Bill Clinton

"Parents should be encouraged to read to their children, and teachers should be equipped with all available techniques for teaching literacy, so the varying needs and capacities of individual kids can be taken into account."

- Hugh Mackay

CONTENTS

CHAPTER I

THE ARRIVAL

"Is this the station, Gran'pa Jim?" inquired a young girl, as the train began to slow up.

"I think so, Mary Louise," replied the handsome old gentleman addressed.

"It does look very promising, does it?" she continued, glancing eagerly out of the window.

"The station? No, my dear; but the station isn't Cragg's Crossing, you know; it is merely the nearest railway point to our new home."

The conductor opened their drawing-room door.

"The next stop is Chargrove, Colonel," he said.

"Thank you."

The porter came for their hand baggage and a moment later the long train stopped and the vestibule steps were let down.

If you will refer to the time-table of the D. R. & G. Railway you will find that the station of Chargrove is marked with a character dagger, meaning that trains stop there only to let off passengers or, when properly signaled, to let them on. Mary Louise, during the journey, had noted this fact with misgivings that were by no means relieved when she stepped from the sumptuous train and found before her merely a shed-like structure, open on all sides, that served as station-house.

Colonel Hathaway and his granddaughter stood silently upon the platform of this shed, their luggage beside them, and watched their trunks tumbled out of the baggage car ahead and the train start, gather speed, and go rumbling on its way. Then the girl looked around her to discover that the primitive station was really the only barren spot in the landscape.

For this was no Western prairie country, but one of the oldest settled and most prosperous sections of a great state that had been one of the original thirteen to be represented by a star on our national banner. Chargrove might not be much of a railway station, as it was only eleven miles from a big city, but the country around it was exceedingly beautiful. Great oaks and maples stood here and there, some in groups and some in stately solitude; the land was well fenced and carefully cultivated; roads—smooth or rutty—led in every direction; flocks and herds were abundant; half hidden by hills or splendid groves peeped the roofs of comfortable farmhouses that evidenced the general prosperity of the community.

"Uncle Eben is late, isn't he, Gran'pa Jim?" asked the girl, as her eyes wandered over the pretty, peaceful scene.

Colonel Hathaway consulted his watch.

"Our train was exactly on time," he remarked, "which is

more than can be said for old Eben. But I think, Mary Louise, I now see an automobile coming along the road. If I am right, we have not long to wait."

He proved to be right, for presently a small touring car came bumping across the tracks and halted at the end of the platform on which they stood. It was driven by an old colored man whose hair was snow white but who sprang from his seat with the agility of a boy when Mary Louise rushed forward with words of greeting.

"My, Uncle Ebe, but it's good to see you again!" she exclaimed, taking both his dusky hands in her own and shaking them cordially. "How is Aunt Polly, and how is your 'rheum'tics'?"

"Rheum'tics done gone foh good, Ma'y Weeze," he said, his round face all smiles. "Dis shuah am one prosterous country foh health. Nobuddy sick but de invahlids, an' dey jus' 'magines dey's sick, dat's all."

"Glad to see you, Uncle," said the Colonel. "A little late, eh? —as usual. But perhaps you had a tire change."

"No, seh, Kun'l, no tire change. I was jus' tryin' to hurry 'long dat lazy Joe Brennan, who's done comin' foh de trunks. Niggehs is slow, Kun'l, dey ain't no argyment 'bout dat, but when a white man's a reg'leh loaf eh, seh, dey ain' no niggeh kin keep behind him."

"Joe Brennan is coming, then?"

"Dat's right, Kun'l; he's comin'. Done start befoh daylight, in de lumbeh-wagin. But when I done ketch up wi' dat Joe—a mile 'n' a half away—he won't lis'n to no reason. So I dodged on ahead to tell you-uns dat Joe's on de way."

"How far is it from here to Cragg's Crossing, then?" inquired Mary Louise.

"They call it ten miles," replied her grandfather, "but I imagine it's nearer twelve."

"And this is the nearest railway station?"

"Yes, the nearest. But usually the Crossing folks who own motor cars drive to the city to take the trains. We alighted here because in our own case it was more convenient and pleasant than running into the city and out again, and it will save us time."

"We be home in half'n hour, mos' likely," added Uncle Eben, as he placed the suit cases and satchels in the car. Colonel Hathaway and Mary Louise followed and took their seats.

"Is it safe to leave our trunks here?" asked the girl.

"Undoubtedly," replied her grandfather. "Joe Brennan will doubtless arrive before long and, really, there is no person around to steal them."

"I've an idea I shall like this part of the country," said Mary Louise musingly, as they drove away.

"I am confident you will, my dear."

"Is Cragg's Crossing as beautiful as this?"

"I think it more beautiful."

"And how did you happen to find it, Gran'pa Jim? It seems as isolated as can be."

"A friend and I were taking a motor trip and lost our way. A farmer told us that if we went to Cragg's Crossing we would find a good road to our destination. We went there, following the man's directions, and encountered beastly roads but found a perfect gem of a tiny, antiquated town which seems to have been forgotten or overlooked by map-makers, automobile guides and tourists. My friend had difficulty in getting me away from the town, I was so charmed with it. Before I left I had discovered, by dint of patient inquiry, a furnished house to let, and you know, of course, that I promptly secured the place for the summer. That's the whole story, Mary Louise."

"It is interesting," she remarked. "As a result of your famous discovery you sent down Uncle Eben and Aunt Polly, with our car and a lot of truck you thought we might need, and now—when all is ready—you and I have come to take possession."

"Rather neatly arranged, I think," declared the Colonel, with satisfaction.

"Do you know anything about the history of the place, Gran'pa, or of the people who live in your tiny, forgotten town?"

"Nothing whatever. I imagine there are folks Cragg's Crossing who have never been a dozen miles away from it since they were born. The village boasts a 'hotel'—the funniest little inn you can imagine—where we had an excellent home-cooked meal; and there is one store and a blacksmith's shop, one church and one schoolhouse. These, with half a dozen ancient and curiously assorted residences, constitute the shy and retiring town of Cragg's Crossing. Ah, think we have found Joe Brennan."

Uncle Eben drew up beside a rickety wagon drawn by two sorry nags who just now were engaged in cropping grass from the roadside. On the seat half reclined a young man who was industriously eating an apple. He wore a blue checked shirt open at the throat, overalls, suspenders and a straw hat that had weathered many seasons of sunshine and rain. His feet were encased in heavy boots and his bronzed face betokened an out-of-door life. There are a million countrymen in the United States just like Joe Brennan in outward appearance.

Joe did not stop munching; he merely stared as the automobile stopped beside him.

"Say, you Joe!" shouted Uncle Eben indignatly, "wha' foh yo' done sett'n' heah?"

"Rest'n'," said Joe Brennan, taking another bite from his apple.

"Ain't yo' gwine git dem trunks home to-day?" demanded the old darkey.

Joe seemed to consider this question carefully before he ventured to commit himself. Then he looked at Colonel Hathaway and said:

"What I want t' know, Boss, is whether I'm hired by the hour, er by the day?"

"Didn't Uncle Eben tell you?"

"Naw, he didn't. He jes' said t' go git the trunks an' he'd gimme a dollar fer the trip."

"Well, that seems to settle the question, doesn't it!"

Edith Van Dyne

"Not quite, Boss. I be'n thinkin' it over, on the way, an' a dollar's too pesky cheap fer this trip. Sometimes I gits twenty-five cents a hour fer haulin' things, an' this looks to me like a day's work."

"If you made good time," said Colonel Hathaway, "you might do it easily in four hours."

Joe shook his head.

"Not me, sir," he replied. "I hain't got the constitution fer it. An' them hosses won't trot 'less I lick 'em, an' ef I lick 'em I'm guilty o' cru'lty ter animals—includin' myself. No, Boss, the job's too cheap, so I guess I'll give it up an' go home."

"But you're nearly at the station now," protested the Colonel.

"I know; but it's half a mile fu'ther an' the hosses is tired. I guess I'll go home."

"Oh, Gran'pa!" whispered Mary Louise, "it'll never do to leave our trunks lying there by the railroad tracks."

The Colonel eyed Joe thoughtfully.

"If you were hired by the day," said he, "I suppose you would do a day's work?"

"I'd hev to," admitted Joe. "That's why I 'asked ye how about it. Jes' now it looks to me like I ain't hired at all. The black man said he'd gimme a dollar fer the trunks, that's all."

"How much do you charge a day?" asked the Colonel.

"Dollar 'n' a quarter's my reg'lar price, an' I won't take no less," asserted Joe.

Mary Louise nearly laughed outright, but the Colonel frowned and said:

"Joe Brennan, you've got me at your mercy. I'm going to hire you by the day, at a dollar and a quarter, and as your time now belongs to me I request you to go at once for those trunks. You will find them just beyond the station."

The man's face brightened. He tossed away the core of his apple and jerked the reins to make the horses hold up their heads.

"A bargain's a bargain, Boss," he remarked cheerfully, "so I'll get them air trunks to yer house if it takes till midnight."

"Very good," said the Colonel. "Drive on, Uncle."

The old servant started the motor.

"Dat's what I calls downright robbery, Kun'l," he exclaimed, highly incensed. "Didn't I ask de stoahkeepeh what to pay Joe Brennen foh bringin' oveh dem trunks, an' didn't he say a dolleh is big pay foh such-like a trip? If we's gwine live in dis town, where day don' un'stand city prices an' de high cost o' livin' yit, we gotta hol' 'em down an' keep 'em from speckilatin' with us, or else we'll spile 'em fer de time when we's gone away."

"Very true, Uncle. Has Joe a competitor?"

Uncle Eben reflected.

"Ef he has, Kun'l, I ain't seen it," he presently replied; "but I guess all he's got is dat lumbeh-wagin."

Mary Louise had enjoyed the controversy immensely and

was relieved by the promise of the trunks by midnight. For the first time in her life the young orphaned girl was to play housekeeper for her grandfather and surely one of her duties was to see that the baggage was safely deposited in their new home.

This unknown home in an unknown town had an intense fascination for her just now. Her grandfather had been rather reticent in his description of the house he had rented at Cragg's Crossing, merely asserting it was a "pretty place" and ought to make them a comfortable home for the summer. Nor had the girl questioned him very closely, for she loved to "discover things" and be surprised—whether pleasurably or not did not greatly interfere with the thrill.

The motor took them speedily along a winding way to Cragg's Crossing, a toy town that caused Mary Louise to draw a long breath of delight at first sight. The "crossing" of two country roads had probably resulted, at some far-back period, in farmers' building their residences on the four corners, so as to be neighborly. Farm hands or others built little dwellings adjoining—not many of them, though—and some unambitious or misdirected merchant erected a big frame "store" and sold groceries, dry goods and other necessities of life not only to the community at the Crossing but to neighboring farmers. Then someone started the little "hotel," mainly to feed the farmers who came to the store to trade or the "drummers" who visited it to sell goods. A church and a schoolhouse naturally followed, in course of time, and then, as if its destiny were fulfilled, the sleepy little town—ten miles from the nearest railway—gradually settled into the comatose state in which Colonel Hathaway and his granddaughter now found it.

CHAPTER II

THE KENTON PLACE

The tiny town, however, was not all that belonged to the Cragg's Crossing settlement. Barely a quarter of a mile away from the village a stream with beautifully wooded banks ran diagonally through the countryside. It was called a "river" by the natives, but it was more of a creek; halfway between a small rivulet and a brook, perhaps. But its banks afforded desirable places for summer residences, several of which had been built by well-to-do families, either retired farmers or city people who wished for a cool and quiet place in which to pass the summer months.

These residences, all having ample grounds and facing the creek on either side, were sufficiently scattered to be secluded, and it was to one of the most imposing of these that Uncle Eben guided the automobile. He crossed the creek on a primitive but substantial bridge, turned to the right, and the first driveway led to the house that was to be Mary Louise's temporary home.

"This is lovely!" exclaimed the girl, as they rolled up a winding drive edged by trees and shrubbery, and finally drew up before the entrance of a low and rambling but quite modern house. There was Aunt Polly, her round black face all smiles, standing on the veranda to greet them, and Mary Louise sprang from the car first to hug the old servant— Uncle Eben's spouse—and then to run in to investigate the establishment, which seemed much finer than she had dared to imagine it.

The main building was of two stories, but the wings, several of which jutted out in various directions, were one story in height, somewhat on the bungalow plan. There was a good-sized stable in connection—now used as a garage—and down among the oaks toward the river an open pavilion had been built. All the open spaces were filled with flowers and ferns, in beds and borders, and graveled paths led here and there in a very enticing way. But the house was now the chief fascination and the other details Mary Louise gleaned by sundry glances from open windows as she rambled from room to room.

At luncheon, which Aunt Polly served as soon as her young mistress could be coaxed from her tour of inspection, the girl said:

"Gran'pa Jim, who owns this place?"

"A Mrs. Joselyn," he replied.

"A young woman?"

"I believe so. It was built by her mother, a Mrs. Kenton, some fifteen years ago, and is still called 'the Kenton Place.' Mrs. Kenton died and her daughter, who married a city man named Joselyn, has used it as a summer home until this year. I think Mrs. Joselyn is a woman of considerable means."

"The furnishings prove that," said Mary Louise. "They're not all in the best of taste, but they are plentiful and meant to be luxurious. Why doesn't Mrs. Joselyn occupy her home this summer? And why, if she is wealthy, does she rent the place?"

"Those are problems I am unable to solve, my dear," replied the Colonel with a smile. "When old man Cragg, who is the nearest approach to a real estate agent in the village, told me the place was for rent, I inquired the price and contracted to lease it for the summer. That satisfied me, Mary Louise, but if you wish to inquire into the history and antecedents of the Kenton and Joselyn families, I have no doubt there are plenty of village gossips who can fill your ears full of it."

"Dar's one thing I foun' out, seh," remarked Uncle Eben, who always served at table and was not too diffident to join in the conversation of his betters, at times; "dis Joselyn man done dis'pear—er run away—er dig out, somehow—an' he missus is mos' plumb crazy 'bout it."

"When did that happen?" asked Mary Louise.

"'Bout Chris'mas time, de stoahkeepah say. Nobody don't like him down heah, 'cause he put on a 'strord'nary 'mount o' airs an' didn't mix wid de town people, nohow. De stoahkeepeh t'inks Marse Joselyn am crooked-like an' done squandeh a lot o' he wife's money befoh he went."

"Perhaps," said Mary Louise musingly, "that is why the poor woman is glad to rent this house. I wish, however, we had gotten it for a more pleasant reason."

"Don't pay attention to Eben's chatter, my dear," advised her grandfather. "His authority seems to be the ancient store-keeper, whom I saw but once and didn't fancy. He looks like an old owl, in those big, horn-rimmed spectacles."

"Dat stoahkeepeh ain' no owl, Kun'l," asserted Uncle Eben earnestly. "He done know all dey is to know 'roun' dese diggin's, an' a lot moah, too. An' a owl is a mighty wise bird, Kun'l, ef I do say it, an' no disrespec'; so what dat stoahkeepeh say I's boun' to take notice of."

Mary Louise spent the afternoon in examining her new possession and "getting settled." For—wonder of wonders! —Joe Brennan arrived with the trunks at three o'clock, some nine hours before the limit of midnight. The Colonel, as he paid the man, congratulated him on making such good time.

"Ya-as," drawled Joe; "I done pretty well, considerin'. But if I hadn't hired out by the day I'd sure be'n a loser. I've be'n a good ten hours goin' fer them trunks, fer I started at five this mornin'; so, if I'd tooken a doller fer the job, I'd only made ten cents a hour, my price bein' twenty-five. But, as it is," he added with pride, "I git my reg'lar rate of a dollar 'n' a quarter a day."

"Proving that it pays to drive a bargain," commented the Colonel.

Mary Louise unpacked Gran'pa Jim's trunk first and put his room in "apple-pie order," as Aunt Polly admiringly asserted. Then she settled her own pretty room, held a conference with her servants about the meals and supplies, and found it was then time to dress for dinner. She was not yet old enough to find household duties a bore, so the afternoon had been delightfully spent.

Early after breakfast the next morning, however, Mary Louise started out to explore the grounds of her domain. The day was full of sunshine and the air laden with fragrance of flowers—a typical May morning. Gran'pa Jim would, of course, read for an hour or two and smoke his pipe; he drew a chair upon the broad veranda for this very purpose; but the girl had the true pioneer spirit of discovery and wanted to know exactly what her five acres contained.

The water was doubtless the prime attraction in such a neighborhood. Mary Louise made straight for the river bank and found the shallow stream—here scarce fifty feet in width—rippling along over its stony bed, which was a full fifty feet wider than the volume of water then required. When the spring freshets were on perhaps the stream reached its banks, but in the summer months it was usually subdued as now. The banks were four feet or more above the rabble of stones below, and close to the bank, facing the river on her side, Mrs. Kenton had built a pretty pavilion with ample seats and room for half a dozen wicker chairs and a table, where one could sit and overlook the water. Mary Louise fervently blessed the old lady for this idea and at once seated herself in the pavilion while she examined at leisure the scene spread out before her.

Trees hid all the neighboring residences but one. Just across the river and not far from its bank stood a small, weather-beaten cottage that was in sharp contrast with the rather imposing Kenton residence opposite. It was not well kept, nor even picturesque. The grounds were unattractive. A woodpile stood in the front yard; the steps leading to the little porch had rotted away and had been replaced by a plank—rather unsafe unless one climbed it carefully, Mary Louise thought. There were time-worn shades to the windows, but no curtains. A pane of glass had been broken in the dormer window and replaced by a folded newspaper tacked over it. Beside the porch door stood a washtub on edge; a few scraggly looking chickens wandered through the yard; if not an abode of poverty it was surely a place where careless indifference to either beauty or the comfort of orderly living prevailed.

So much Mary Louise had observed, wondering why Mrs. Kenton had not bought the cottage and torn it down, since it was a blot on the surrounding landscape, when she saw the door open and a man come out. She gave a little gasp of astonishment as her eyes followed this man, who slowly took the path to the bridge, from whence the road led into the village.

CHAPTER III

THE FOLKS ACROSS THE RIVER

Her first glance told the girl that here was a distinctly unusual personage. His very appearance was quaint enough to excite comment from a stranger. It must have been away back in the revolutionary days when men daily wore coats cut in this fashion, straight across the waist-line in front and with two long tails flapping behind. Modern "dress coats" were much like it, to be sure, but this was of a faded blue-bottle color and had brass buttons and a frayed velvet collar on it. His trousers were tight-fitting below the knee and he wore gaiters and a wide-brimmed silk hat that rivaled his own age and had doubtless seen happier days.

Mary Louise couldn't see all these details from her seat in the pavilion across the river, but she was near enough to observe the general effect of the old man's antiquated costume and it amazed her.

Yes, he was old, nearly as ancient as his apparel, the girl decided; but although he moved with slow deliberation his gait was not feeble, by any means. With hands clasped behind him and head slightly bowed, as if in meditation, he paced the length of the well-worn path, reached the bridge and disappeared down the road toward the village.

Edith Van Dyne

"That," said a voice beside her, "is the Pooh-Bah of Cragg's Crossing. It is old Cragg himself."

Gran'pa Jim was leaning against the outer breast of the pavilion, book in hand.

"You startled me," she said, "but no more than that queer old man did. Was the village named after him, Gran'pa?"

"I suppose so; or after his father, perhaps, for the place seems even older than old Cragg. He has an 'office' in a bare little room over the store, and I rented this place from him. Whatever his former fortunes may have been—and I imagine the Craggs once owned all the land about here—old Hezekiah seems reduced to a bare existence."

"Perhaps," suggested Mary Louise, "he inherited those clothes with the land, from his father. Isn't it an absurd costume, Gran'pa Jim? And in these days of advanced civilization, too! Of course old Hezekiah Cragg is not strong mentally or he would refuse to make a laughingstock of himself in that way."

Colonel Hathaway stared across the river for a time without answering. Then he said:

"I do not think the natives here laugh at him, although I remember they called him 'Old Swallowtail' when I was directed to him as the only resident real estate agent. I found the old man quite shrewd in driving a bargain and thoroughly posted on all the affairs of the community. However, he is not a gossip, but inclined to be taciturn. There is a fathomless look in his eyes and he is cold and unresponsive. Country life breeds strange characteristics in some people. The whimsical dress and mannerisms of old Mr. Cragg would not be tolerated in the cities, while here they seem regarded with unconcern because they have become familiar. I was rather, pleased with his personality because he is the Cragg of Cragg's Crossing. How much of the original plot of land he still owns I don't know."

"Why, he lives in that hovel!" said the girl.

"So it seems, although he may have been merely calling there."

"He fits the place," she declared. "It's old and worn and neglected, just as he and his clothes are. I'd be sorry, indeed, to discover that Mr. Cragg lives anywhere else."

The Colonel, his finger between the leaves of the book he held, to mark the place where he was reading, nodded somewhat absently and started to turn away. Then he paused to ask anxiously:

"Does this place please you, my dear?"

"Ever so much, Gran'pa Jim!" she replied with enthusiasm, leaning from her seat inside the pavilion to press a kiss upon his bare gray head. "I've a sense of separation from all the world, yet it seems good to be hidden away in this forgotten nook. Perhaps I wouldn't like it for always, you know, but for a summer it is simply delightful. We can rest—and rest— and rest!—and be as cozy as can be."

Again the old gentleman nodded, smiling at the girl this time. They were good chums, these two, and what pleased one usually pleased the other.

Colonel Hathaway had endured a sad experience recently and his handsome old face still bore the marks of past mental suffering. His only daughter, Beatrice Burrows, who was the mother of Mary Louise, had been indirectly responsible for the Colonel's troubles, but her death had lifted the burden; her little orphaned girl, to whom no blame could be attached, was very dear to "Gran'pa Jim's" heart. Indeed, she was all he now had to love and care for and he continually planned to promote her happiness and to educate her to become a noble woman. Fortunately he had saved considerable money from the remains of an immense estate he had once possessed and so was able to do anything for his grandchild that he desired. In New York and elsewhere Colonel James Hathaway had a host of influential friends, but he was shy of meeting them since his late unpleasant experiences.

Mary Louise, for her part, was devotedly attached to her grandfather and preferred his society to that of any other person. As the erect form of the old gentleman sauntered away through the trees she looked after him affectionately and wagged her little head with hearty approval.

"This is just the place for Gran'pa Jim," she mused. "There's no one to bother him with questions or sympathy and he can live as quietly as he likes and read those stuffy old books— the very name 'classics' makes me shudder—to his heart's content. He'll grow stronger and happier here, I'm sure."

Then she turned anew to revel in the constantly shifting view of river and woodland that extended panoramically from her seat in the pavilion. As her eyes fell on the old cottage opposite she was surprised to see a dishpan sail through the open window, to fall with a clatter of broken dishes on the hard ground of the yard. A couple of dish-towels followed, and then a broom and a scrubbing-brush—all tossed out in an angry, energetic way that scattered them in every direction. Then on the porch appeared the form of a small girl, poorly dressed in a shabby gingham gown, who danced up and down for a moment as if mad with rage and then, observing the washtub, gave it a kick which sent it rolling off the porch to join the other utensils on the ground.

Next, the small girl looked around her as if seeking more inanimate things upon which to vent her anger, but finding none she dashed into the cottage and soon reappeared with a much-worn straw hat which she jammed on her flaxen head and then, with a determined air, walked down the plank and marched up the path toward the bridge—the same direction that old Cragg had taken a short time before.

Mary Louise gave a gasp of amazement. The scene had been dramatic and exciting while it lasted and it needed no explanation whatever. The child had plainly rebelled at enforced drudgery and was going—where?

Mary Louise sprang lightly from her seat and ran through the grounds to their entrance. When she got to the road she sped along until she came to the bridge, reaching one end of it just as the other girl started to cross from the opposite end. Then she stopped and in a moment the two met.

"Where are you going?" asked Mary Louise, laying a hand on the child's arm as she attempted to pass her.

"None o' yer business," was the curt reply.

"Oh, it is, indeed," said Mary Louise, panting a little from her run. "I saw you throw things, a minute ago, so I guess you mean to run away."

The girl turned and stared at her.

"I don't know ye," said she. "Never saw ye before. Where'd ye come from anyway?"

"Why, my grandfather and I have taken the Kenton house for the summer, so we're to be your neighbors. Of course, you know, we must get acquainted."

"Ye kin be neighbors to my Gran'dad, if ye like, but not to me. Not by a ginger cookie! I've done wi' this place fer good an' all, I hev, and if ye ever see me here ag'in my name ain't Ingua Scammel!"

"Here; let's sit down on the bridge and talk it over," proposed Mary Louise. "There's plenty of time for you to run away, if you think you'd better. Is Mr. Cragg your grandfather, then?"

"Yes, Ol' Swallertail is. 'Ol' Humbug' is what *I* calls him."

"Not to his face, do you?"

"I ain't so foolish. He's got a grip on him like a lobster, an' when he's mad at me he grips my arm an' twists it till I holler. When Gran'dad's aroun' you bet I hev to knuckle down, er I gits the worst of it."

"So he's cruel, is he?"

"Uh-huh. Thet is, he's cruel when I riles him, as I got a habit o' doin'. When things runs smooth, Gran'dad ain't so bad; but I ain't goin' to stand that slave life no longer, I ain't. I've quit fer good."

"Wherever you go," said Mary Louise gently, "you will have to work for someone. Someone, perhaps, who treats you worse than your grandfather does. No one else is obliged to care for you in any way, so perhaps you're not making a wise change."

"I ain't, eh?"

"Perhaps not. Have you any other relatives to go to?"

"No."

"Or any money?"

"Not a red cent."

"Then you'll have to hire out as a servant. You're not big enough or strong enough to do much, so you'll search a long time before you find work, and that means being hungry and without shelter. I know more of the world than you do, Ingua—what an odd name you have!—and I honestly think you are making a mistake to run away from your own grandfather."

The girl stared into the water in sullen silence for a time. Mary Louise got a good look at her now and saw that her freckled face might be pretty if it were not so thin and drawn. The hands lying on her lap were red and calloused with housework and the child's whole appearance indicated neglect, from the broken-down shoes to the soiled and tattered dress. She seemed to be reflecting, for after a while she gave a short, bitter laugh at the recollection of her late exhibition of temper and said:

"It's too late to back, down now. I've busted the dishes an' smashed things gen'rally."

"That *is* bad," said Mary Louise; "but it might be worse. Mr. Cragg can buy more dishes."

"Oh, he can, can he? Where's the money comin' from?"

"Is he poor?"

"He ain't got no money, if that's what ye mean. That's what he says, anyhow. Says it were a godsend you folks rented that house of him, 'cause it'll keep us in corn bread an' pork for six months, ef we're keerful. Bein' keerful means that he'll eat the pork an' I gits a chunk o' corn bread now an' then."

"Dear me!" exclaimed Mary Louise in a distressed voice. "Don't you get enough to eat?"

"Oh, I manages it somehow," declared Ingua, with indifference. "I be'n swipin' one egg a day fer weeks an' weeks. Gran'dad says he'll trim me good an' plenty if he catches me eatin' eggs, 'cause all that our chickens lays he takes down to the store an' sells. But he ain't home daytimes, to count what eggs is laid, an' so I watches out an' grabs one a day. He's mighty cute, I tell ye, Gran'dad is; but he ain't cute enough to catch me at the egg-swipin'."

Mary Louise was greatly shocked. Really, she decided, something must be done for this poor child. Looking at the matter from Ingua's report, the smashing of the dishes might prove serious. So she said:

"Come, dear, let's go together to your house and see if we can't restore the damage."

But the girl shook her head.

"Noth'n' can't mend them busted dishes," she said, "an' when Gran'dad sees 'em he'll hev a fit. That's why I did it; I wanted to show him I'd had revenge afore I quit him cold. He won't be home till night, but I gotta be a long way off, afore then, so's he can't ketch me."

"Give it up," suggested Mary Louise. "I've come here to live all summer, Ingua, and now that we're friends I'm going to help you to get along more comfortably. We will have some splendid times together, you and I, and you will be a good deal better off than wandering among strangers who don't care for you."

The girl turned and looked into Mary Louise's face long and earnestly. Her eyes wandered to her neatly arranged hair, to the white collar at her throat, then down to her blue serge dress and her dainty shoes. But mostly she looked straight into the eyes of her new friend and found there sincerity and evident good will. So she sighed deeply, cast a glance at her own bedraggled attire, and said:

"We ain't much alike, us two, but I guess we kin be friends. Other girls has come here, to the rich people's houses, but they all stuck up their noses at me. You're the first that's ever give me a word."

"All girls are not alike, you know," responded Mary Louise cheerfully. "So now, let's go to your house and see what damage has been done."

CHAPTER IV

GETTING ACQUAINTED

The two girls had been sitting on the edge of the bridge, but Mary Louise now rose and took Ingua's arm in her own, leading the reluctant child gently toward the path. It wasn't far to the old cottage and when they reached the yard Ingua laughed again at the scene of disorder.

"It's a'most a pity Gran'dad can't see it," she chuckled. "He'd be so crazy he'd hev them claws o' his'n 'round my throat in a jiffy."

Mary Louise drew back, startled.

"Did he ever do that?" she asked.

"Only once; but that time near ended me. It were a long time ago, an' he was sorry, I guess, 'cause he bought me a new dress nex' day—an' new shoes! I ain't had any since," she added disconsolately, "so the other day I asked him wasn't it about time he choked me ag'in."

"What did he say to that?"

"Jes' growled at me. Gran'dad's got a awful temper when he's good an' riled, but usual' he's still as a mouse. Don't say a word to me fer days together, sometimes. Once I saw him—"

She suddenly checked herself and cast an uneasy, sidelong glance at her companion. Mary Louise was rolling the washtub back to the stoop.

"The only thing that will bother us, Ingua," she said, "is those dishes. Let us try to count the broken ones. Do you know how many there were?"

"Sure I do," answered the girl, removing the battered dishpan from the heap of crockery. "Two plates, two cups-'n'-saucers, a oatmeal dish, a bread plate an' the pork platter. Gee! what a smash. One cup's whole—an' the oatmeal dish. The rest is gone-up."

"I'm going to dig a hole and bury the broken pieces," said Mary Louise. "Have you a spade?"

"There's an ol' shovel. But it won't do no good to bury of 'em. Gran'dad he counts ev'ry piece ev'ry day. He counts ev'ry thing, from the grains of salt to the chickens. Say, once I tried to play a trick on him. I'd got so hungry fer meat I jes' couldn't stand it, so one day I killed a chick'n, thinkin' he wouldn't miss it. My—my! Wha' d'ye s'pose? Say, ye never told me yer name yit."

"I am Mary Louise Burrows."

"Highflyin' name, ain't it? Well, I killed thet chick'n, an' cut it up an' fried it, an' et jes' a leg an' a wing, an' hid the rest under my bed in the peak up there, where Ol' Swallertail never goes. All the feathers an' the head I buried, an' I cleaned up the hatchet an' the fry-in'-pan so's there wasn't a smitch of anything left to prove I'd murdered one o' them

Edith Van Dyne

chicks. I was feelin' kinder chirky when Gran'dad come home, 'cause I thought he'd never find out. But what did the ol' vill'n do but begin to sniff aroun'; an' he sniffed an' he sniffed till he says: 'Ingua, what chick'n did ye kill, an' why did ye kill it?'"

"'Yer crazy,' says I. 'What're ye talkin' 'bout?'"

"Then he gives me one sour look an' marches out to count the chick'ns, an' when he comes back he says: 'It's the brown pullet with white on the wings. It were worth forty cents, an' forty cents'll buy ten pounds o' oatmeal. Where's the chick'n, girl?' 'Et up,' says I. 'Yer lyin',' says he. 'Go git it! Hustle!'

"Well, I saw his claws beginnin' to work an' it scared me stiff. So I goes to my room an' brings down the chick'n, an' he eyes it quiet-like fer a long time an' then eats some fer his supper. The rest he locks up in the cupboard that he allus carries the key to. Say, Mary Louise, I never got another taste o' that chick'n as long as it lasted! Ol' Swallertail et it all himself, an' took a week to do it."

During this recital the broom and mop and scrubbing-brush had been picked up and restored to their proper places. Then the two girls got out the old shovel and buried the broken dishes in a far corner of the yard, among high weeds. Mary Louise tried to get the dents out of the old dishpan, but succeeded only indifferently. It was so battered through long use, however, that Ingua thought the "jams" would not be noticed.

"Next," said Mary Louise, "we must replace the broken pieces. I suppose they sell dishes at the village store, do they not?"

"That's where these come from—long ago," replied Ingua;

"but dishes cost money."

"I've a little money in my purse; enough for that, I'm sure. Will you go to town with me?"

Ingua stared at her as if bewildered. The proposition was wholly beyond her understanding. But she replied to her new friend's question, saying slowly:

"No; I won't go. Ol' Swallertail'd skin me alive if he caught me in the village."

"Then I'll go alone; and I'll soon be back, though I must run over to my own house first, to get my purse and my hat. Let me have one of the cups for a sample, Ingua."

She left the child sitting on the plank runway and looking rather solemn and thoughtful. Mary Louise was somewhat fearful that she might run away in her absence, so she hurried home and from there walked into the village, a tramp easily accomplished in ten minutes.

The store was the biggest building in town, but not very big at that. It was "clapboarded" and two stories in height, the upper floor being used by Sol Jerrems, the storekeeper, as a residence, except for two little front rooms which he rented, one to Miss Huckins, the dressmaker and milliner, who slept and ate in her shop, and the other to Mr. Cragg. A high platform had been built in front of the store, for the convenience of farmer customers in muddy weather, and there were steps at either end of the platform for the use of pedestrians.

When Mary Louise entered the store, which was cluttered with all sorts of goods, not arranged in very orderly manner, there were several farmers present. But old Sol had his eye on her in an instant and shuffled forward to wait upon her.

"I want some crockery, please," she said.

He looked at the sample cup and led her to a corner of the room where a jumble of dishes crowded a single shelf.

"I take it you're one o' them new folks at the Kenton Place," he remarked.

"Yes," said she.

"Thought ther' was plenty o' dishes in that place," continued Mr. Jerrems, in a friendly tone. "But p'r'aps ye don't want the black folks t' eat off'n the same things ye do yerselves."

Mary Louise ignored this speech and selected the dishes she wanted. She had measured the broken platter and found another of the same size. Old Sol wouldn't sell a saucer without a cup, explaining that the two always went together: "the cup to hold the stuff an' the saucer to drink it out'n." Without argument, however, the girl purchased what she wanted. It was heavy, cheap ware of the commonest kind, but she dared not substitute anything better for it.

Then she went to the grocery counter and after considering what Ingua might safely hide and eat in secret she bought a tin of cooked corned beef, another of chipped beef, one of deviled ham and three tins of sardines. Also she bought a basket to carry her purchases in and although old Sol constantly sought to "pump" her concerning her past life, present history and future prospects, she managed to evade successfully his thirst for information. No doubt the fellow was a great gossip, as old Eben had declared, but Mary Louise knew better than to cater to this dangerous talent.

The proprietor accompanied her to the door and she drew back, hesitating, as she observed an old man in a bottle-blue swallowtail coat pace in deliberate, dignified manner along the opposite side of the street.

"Who is that?" she asked, as an excuse for not going out until Ingua's grandfather had passed from sight.

"That? Why, that's Ol' Swallertail, otherwise Hezekiah Cragg, one o' our most interestin' citizens," replied Sol, glad of the chance to talk.

"Does he own Cragg's Crossing?" asked Mary Louise.

"Mercy, no! He owned a lot of it once, though, but that were afore my time. Sold it out an' squandered the money, I guess, for he lives like a rat in a hole. Mebbe, though, he's got some hid away; that's what some o' the folks here whispers—folks that's likely to know. But, if that's a fact, he's got a streak o' miser in him, for he don't spend more'n the law allows."

"He may have lost the money in speculations," suggested the girl.

"Say, ye've hit the nail square on the head!" he exclaimed admiringly. "Them's my own opinions to a T. I've told the boys so a hunderd times, but they can't git it. Wasn't Ol' Swal-lertail hand-in-glove wi' that slick Mister Joselyn, who they say has run away an' left his pore wife in the lurch? That's how you got a chance to rent the Kenton house. Joselyn were slick as butter, an' high-strung. Wouldn't hobnob with any o' us but Ol' Swallertail, an' that's why I think Cragg was investin' money with him. Joselyn he came down here three year ago, havin' married Annabel Kenton in the winter, an' the way he swelled aroun' were a caution to snakes. But the pore devil run his rope an' lit out. Where he skipped to, I dunno. Nobuddy seems to know, not even his wife. But they say she didn't hev enough money left to count, an' by the glum looks o' Ol' Swallertail I'm guessin' he got nipped too."

"How long ago was that?" asked Mary Louise.

"Some time 'bout last Christmas, they say. Anyhow, that's when his wife missed him an' set up a hunt that didn't do no good. She came down here with red eyes an' tramped 'round in the deep snow askin' questions. But, sakes, Ned Joselyn wouldn't 'a' come to an out-o'-the-way place like this; we didn't never suit his style, ye see; so poor Ann Kenton—whose misfortun' made her Mrs. Ned Joselyn—cried an' wailed fer a day er two an' then crep' back to the city like a whipped dog. Funny how women'll care fer a wuthless, ne'er-do-well chap that happens to be good-lookin', ain't it?"

Mary Louise nodded rather absently. However distorted the story might be, it was curious what had become of Mr. Joselyn. But her thoughts reverted to another theme and she asked:

"Hasn't Mr. Cragg a granddaughter?"

"Oh, ye've seen little Ingua Scammel, hev ye? Or mebbe just heard tell of her. She's the cussedest little coal o' fire in seven counties! Keeps Ol' Swallertail guessin' all the time, they say, jes' like her mom, Nan Cragg, did afore her. Gosh, what a woman her mom were! She didn't stay 'round here much, but whenever she run out o' cash an' didn't hev a square meal comin' to her, she camped on Ol' Swallertail an' made him board her. Las' time she come she left her young-un—that's Ingua, ye know—an' the kid's been here ever since; sort of a thorn in the side of ol' Hezekiah, we folks think, though he don't never complain. She ain't more'n twelve or thirteen year old, thet Ingua, but she keeps house fer her gran'dad—what they is to keep, which ain't much. I won't let the kid 'round my store, nohow, 'cause she swipes ev'rything, from dried apples to peanuts, thet she kin lay her hands on."

"Perhaps she is hungry," said Mary Louise, defending her new friend.

"Like enough. But I ain't feedin' starvin' kids, 'Tain't my business. If Ol' Swallertail don't feed her enough, thet's *his* lookout. I've warned him if she sets foot in this store I'll charge him ten cents, jes' fer safety, so he keeps her out. He's slick, Ol' Swallertail is, an' silent-like an' secret in all he does an' says; but he's got to git up earlier in the mornin' to git the best o' Sol Jerrems, he er his kid, either one."

As Mr. Cragg had now vanished from sight up the street, Mary Louise ventured out and after a brisk walk deposited her basket on the stoop of the Cragg cottage, where Ingua still sat, swinging her feet pensively, as if she had not stirred since Mary Louise had left her.

Edith Van Dyne

CHAPTER V

MARY LOUISE BECOMES A PEACEMAKER

"Here are the dishes, exactly like the broken ones," reported Mary Louise in a jubilant tone as she set down her heavy basket. "Let us go in and wash them, Ingua, and put them away where they belong."

The child followed her into the house. All her former pent-up energy seemed to have evaporated. She moved in a dull sort of way that betokened grim resignation.

"I've be'n plannin' fer months to make a run fer it," she remarked as she washed the new dishes and Mary Louise wiped them dry, "an' just when I'd mustered up courage to do the trick, along comes *you* an' queered the whole game."

"You'll thank me for that, some day, Ingua. Aren't you glad, even now, that you have a home and shelter?"

"I ain't tickled to death about it. Home!" with a scornful glance around the room, barren of all comforts. "A graveyard's a more cheerful place, to my notion."

"We must try to make it pleasanter, dear. I'm going to get acquainted with Mr. Cragg and coax him to brighten things up some, and buy you some new clothes, and take better care of you."

Ingua fell back on a stool, fairly choking twixt amazement and derision.

"You! Coax Ol' Swallertail? Make him spend money on *me!* Say, if ye wasn't a stranger here, Mary Louise, I'd jes' laugh; but bein' as how yer a poor innercent, I'll only say ther' ain't no power on earth kin coax Gran'dad to do anything better than to scowl an' box my ears. You don't know him, but *I* do."

"Meantime," said Mary Louise, refusing to argue the point, "here are some little things for you to hide away, and to eat whenever you please," and she took from the basket the canned goods she had bought and set them in an enticing row upon the table.

Ingua stared at the groceries and then stared at Mary Louise. Her wan face flushed and then grew hard.

"Ye bought them fer *me?*" she asked.

"Yes; so you won't have to steal eggs to satisfy your natural hunger."

"Well, ye kin take the truck away ag'in. An' you'd better go with it," said the girl indignantly. "We may be poor, but we ain't no beggars, an' we don't take charity from nobody."

"But your grandfather—"

"We'll pay our own bills an' buy our own fodder. The Craggs is jus' as good as yer folks, an' I'm a Cragg to the backbone," she cried, her eyes glinting angrily. "If we want to starve, it's none o' yer business, ner nobody else's," and springing up she seized the tins one by one and sent them flying through the window, as she had sent the dishpan and dishes earlier in the morning. "Now, then, foller yer charity an' make yerself scarce!" and she stamped her foot defiantly at Mary Louise, who was dumb with astonishment.

It was hard to understand this queer girl. She had made no objection to replacing the broken dishes, yet a present of food aroused her to violent anger. Her temper was positively something terrible in so small a person and remembering her story of how Old Swallowtail had clenched his talon-like fingers and twisted Ingua's arm till she screamed with pain, Mary Louise could well believe the statement that the child was "a Cragg to the backbone."

But Mary Louise, although only a few years older than Ingua, had had a good deal more experience and was, moreover, a born diplomat. Astonished though she was, she quickly comprehended the peculiar pride exhibited in a refusal to accept food from a stranger and knew she must soothe the girl's outraged spirit of independence if they were to remain friends.

"I guess I'll have to beg your pardon, Ingua," she said quietly. "I was grieved that you are so often hungry, while I have so much more than I need, and the money which I spent was all my own, to do what I liked with. If I were in your place, and you in mine, and we were good chums, as I know we're going to be, I'd be glad to have you help me in any little way you could. True friends, Ingua, share and share alike and don't let any foolish pride come between them."

She spoke earnestly, with a ring of sincerity in her voice that impressed the other girl. Ingua's anger had melted as quickly as it had roused and with sudden impulsiveness she seized

Mary Louise's hands in her own and began to cry.

"I'm as wicked as they make 'em!" she wailed. "I know I am! But I can't help it, Mary Louise; it's borned in me. I want to be friends with ye, but I won't take your charity if I starve. Not now, anyhow. Here; I'll go git the stuff an' put it back in yer basket, an' then ye kin lug it home an' do what ye please with it."

They picked up the cans together, Ingua growing more calm and cheerful each moment. She even laughed at Mary Louise's disappointed expression and said:

"I don't always hev tantrums. This is my bad day; but the devils'll work out o' me by termorrer and I'll be sweet as sugar. I'm sorry; but it's the Cragg blood that sets me crazy, at times."

"Won't you run over and see me?" asked Mary Louise, preparing to go home.

"When?"

"This afternoon."

Ingua shook her head.

"I dastn't," she said. "I gotta hold myself in, the rest o' the day, so's I won't fight with Ol' Swallertail when he comes home. Anyhow, I ain't fit t' show up aroun' yer swell place. That black coon o' yers'd turn me out, if he saw me comin', thinkin' I was a tramp."

Mary Louise had a bright idea.

"I'm going to have tea to-morrow afternoon in that summer-house across the creek," said she. "I will be all alone and if you will come over and join me we'll have a nice visit together. Will you, Ingua?"

"I guess so," was the careless answer. "When ye're ready, jes' wave yer han'ker'cher an if the devils ain't squeezin' my gizzard, like they is to-day, I'll be there in a jiffy."

CHAPTER VI

AFTERNOON TEA

Mary Louise, who possessed a strong sense of humor, that evening at dinner told Gran'pa Jim of her encounter with old Mr. Cragg's granddaughter and related their interview in so whimsical a manner that Colonel Hathaway laughed aloud more than once. But he also looked serious, at times, and when the recital was ended he gravely considered the situation and said:

"I believe, my dear, you have discovered a mine of human interest here that will keep you occupied all summer. It was most fortunate for the poor child that you interpreted her intent to run away from home and foiled it so cleverly. From the little girl's report, that grim and dignified grandsire of hers has another and less admirable side to his character and, unless she grossly exaggerates, has a temper so violent that he may do her a mischief some day."

"I'm afraid of that, too," declared Mary Louise, "especially as the child is so provoking. Yet I'm sure Ingua has a sweeter side to her nature, if it can be developed, and perhaps old Cragg has, too. Do you think, Gran'pa Jim, it would be advisable for me to plead with him to treat his orphaned grandchild more considerately?"

Edith Van Dyne

"Not at present, my dear. I'll make some inquiries concerning Cragg and when we know more about him we can better judge how best to help Ingua. Are you sure that is her name?"

"Yes; isn't it an odd name?"

"Somewhere," said the Colonel, musingly, "I have heard it before, but just now I cannot recollect where. It seems to me, however, that it was a man's name. Do you think the child's mother is dead?"

"I gathered from what Ingua and the storekeeper said that she has simply disappeared."

"An erratic sort of creature, from the vague reports you have heard," commented Gran'pa Jim. "But, whatever her antecedents may have been, there is no reason why Ingua may not be rescued from her dreadful environments and be made to become a quite proper young lady, if not a model one. But that can only result from changing the existing character of her environment, rather than taking her out of them."

"That will be a big task, Gran'pa Jim, and it may prove beyond me, but I'll do the best I can."

He smiled.

"These little attempts to help our fellows," said the Colonel, "not only afford us pleasure but render us stronger and braver in facing our own tribulations, which none, however securely placed, seem able to evade."

Mary Louise gave him a quick, sympathetic glance. He had surely been brave and strong during his own period of tribulation and the girl felt she could rely on his aid in whatever sensible philanthropy she might undertake. She was glad, indeed, to have discovered poor Ingua, for she was too active and of too nervous a temperament to be content simply to "rest" all summer. Rest was good for Gran'pa Jim, just now, but rest pure and simple, with no compensating interest, would soon drive Mary Louise frantic.

She conferred with Aunt Polly the next day and told the faithful black servant something of her plans. So, when the old cook lugged a huge basket to the pavilion for her in the afternoon, and set a small table with snowy linen and bright silver, with an alcohol arrangement for making tea, she said with an air of mystery:

"Don' yo' go open dat bastik, Ma'y 'Weeze, till de time comes fer eatin'. I jes' wants to s'prise yo'—yo' an' dat li'l' pooah girl what gits hungry so much."

So, when Aunt Polly had gone back to the house, Mary Louise arranged her table and then stood up and waved a handkerchief to signal that all was ready.

Soon Ingua appeared in her doorway, hesitated a moment, and then ran down the plank and advanced to the river bank instead of following the path to the bridge. Almost opposite the pavilion Mary Louise noticed that several stones protruded from the surface of the water. They were not in a line, but placed irregularly. However, Ingua knew their lie perfectly and was able to step from one to another until she had quickly passed the water. Then she ran up the dry bed of the river to the bank, where steps led to the top.

"Why, this is fine!" exclaimed Mary Louise, meeting her little friend at the steps. "I'd no idea one could cross the river in that way."

"Oh, we've known 'bout that always," was the reply. "Ned Joselyn used to come to our house ever so many times by the river stones, to talk with Ol' Swallertail, an' Gran'dad used to come over here, to this same summer-house, an' talk with Joselyn."

Mary Louise noticed that the old gingham dress had been washed, ironed and mended—all in a clumsy manner. Ingua's blond hair had also been trained in awkward imitation of the way Mary Louise dressed her own brown locks. The child, observing her critical gaze, exclaimed with a laugh:

"Yes, I've slicked up some. No one'll see me but you, will they?" she added suspiciously.

"No, indeed; we're to be all alone. How do you feel to-day, Ingua?"

"The devils are gone. Gran'dad didn't 'spicion anything las' night an' never said a word. He had one o' his dreamy fits an' writ letters till long after I went to bed. This mornin' he said as ol' Sol Jerrems has raised the price o' flour two cents, so I'll hev to be keerful; but that was all. No rumpus ner anything."

"That's nice," said Mary Louise, leading her, arm in arm, to the pavilion. "Aren't you glad you didn't run away?"

Ingua did not reply. Her eyes, big and round, were taking in every detail of the table. Then they wandered to the big basket and Mary Louise smiled and said:

"The table is set, as you see, but I don't know what we're to have to eat. I asked Aunt Polly to put something in the basket, as I was going to have company, and I'm certain there'll be *enough* for two, whatever it's like. You see, this is a sort of surprise party, for we won't know what we've got until we unpack the basket."

Ingua nodded, much interested.

"Ye said 'tea,'" she remarked, "an' I hain't tasted tea sence Marm left us. But I s'pose somethin' goes with tea?"

"Always. Tea means a lunch, you know, and I'm very hungry because I didn't eat much luncheon at noon. I hope you are hungry, too, Ingua," she added, opening the basket and beginning to place its contents upon the table.

Ingua may have considered a reply unnecessary, for she made none. Her eyes were growing bigger every moment, for here were dainty sandwiches, cakes, jelly, a pot of marmalade, an assortment of cold meats, olives, Saratoga chips, and last of all a chicken pie still warm from the oven —one of those chicken pies that Aunt Polly could make as no one else ever made them.

Even Mary Louise was surprised at the array of eatables. It was a veritable feast. But without comment she made the tea, the water being already boiling, and seating Ingua opposite her at the table she served the child as liberally as she dared, bearing in mind her sensitiveness to "charity."

But Ingua considered this a "party," where as a guest she was entitled to all the good things, and she ate with a ravenous haste that was pitiful, trying the while not to show how hungry she was or how good everything tasted to her.

Mary Louise didn't burden her with conversation during the meal, which she prolonged until the child positively could eat no more. Then she drew their chairs to a place where they had the best view of the river and woodland—with the old Cragg cottage marring the foreground—and said:

"Now we will have a good, long talk together."

Ingua sighed deeply.

"Don't we hev to do the dishes?" she asked.

"No; Aunt Polly will come for them, by and by. All we have to do now is to enjoy your visit, which I hope you will repeat many times while I am living here."

Again the child sighed contentedly.

"I wish ye was goin' ter stay always," she remarked. "You folks is a sight nicer'n that Joselyn tribe. They kep' us stirred up a good deal till Ned—"

She stopped abruptly.

"What were the Joselyns like?" inquired Mary Louise, in a casual tone that was meant to mask her curiosity.

"Well, that's hard to say," answered Ingua thoughtfully. "Ol' Mis' Kenton were a good lady, an' ev'rybody liked her; but after she died Ann Kenton come down here with a new husban', who were Ned Joselyn, an' then things began to happen. Ned was slick as a ban'box an' wouldn't hobnob with nobody, at first; but one day he got acquainted with Ol' Swallertail an' they made up somethin' wonderful. I guess other folks didn't know 'bout their bein' so close, fer they was sly 'bout it, gen'rally. They'd meet in this summer-house, or they'd meet at our house, crossin' the river on the steppin'-stones; but when Ned came over to us Gran'dad allus sent me away an' said he'd skin me if I listened. But one day—No, I mus'n't tell that," she said, checking herself quickly, as a hard look came over her face.

"Why not?" softly asked Mary Louise.

"'Cause if I do I'll git killed, that's why," answered the child, in a tone of conviction.

Something in her manner startled her hearer.

"Who would kill you, Ingua?" she asked.

"Gran'dad would."

"Oh, I'm sure he wouldn't do that, whatever you said."

"Ye don't know Gran'dad, Mary Louise. He'd as lief kill me as look at me, if I give him cause to."

"And he has asked you not to talk about Mr. Joselyn?"

"He tol' me ter keep my mouth shet or he'd murder me an' stick my body in a hole in the yard. An' he'd do it in a minute, ye kin bank on that."

"Then," said Mary Louise, looking troubled, "I advise you not to say anything he has forbidden you to. And, if anything ever happens to you while I'm here, I shall tell Gran'pa Jim to have Mr. Cragg arrested and put in prison."

"Will ye? Will ye—honest?" asked the girl eagerly. "Say! that'll help a lot. If I'm killed, I'll know I'll be revenged."

So tragic was her manner that Mary Louise could have laughed outright had she not felt there was a really serious foundation for Ingua's fears. There was something about the

silent, cold-featured, mysterious old man that led her to
believe he might be guilty of any crime. But, after all, she
reflected, she knew Mr. Cragg's character only from Ingua's
description of it, and the child feared and hated him.

"What does your grandfather do in his office all day?" she
inquired after a long pause.

"Writes letters an' reads the ones he gits, I guess. He don't let
me go to his office."

"Does he get many letters, then?"

"Heaps an' heaps of 'em. You ask Jim Bennett, who brings
the mail bag over from the station ev'ry day."

"Is Jim Bennett the postman?"

"His wife is. Jim lugs the mail 'tween the station an' his own
house—that's the little white house next the church—where
his wife, who's deef-'n'-dumb, runs the postoffice. I know
Jim. He says there's 'bout six letters a year for the farmers
'round here, an' 'bout one a week for Sol Jerrems—which is
mostly bills—an' all the rest belongs to Ol' Swallertail."

Mary Louise was puzzled.

"Has he a business, then?" she asked.

"Not as anybody knows of."

"But why does he receive and answer so many letters?"

"Ye'll hev to guess. I've guessed, myself; but what's the use?
If he was as stingy of postage stamps as he is of pork an'
oatmeal, he wouldn't send a letter a year."

Mary Louise scented a mystery. Mysteries are delightful things to discover, and fascinating to solve. But who would have thought this quiet, retired village harbored a mystery?

"Does your grandfather ever go away from here? Does he travel much?" was her next question.

"He ain't never been out of Cragg's Crossing sence I've knowed him."

"Really," said Mary Louise, "it is perplexing."

Ingua nodded. She was feeling quite happy after her lunch and already counted Mary Louise a warm friend. She had never had a friend before, yet here was a girl of nearly her own age who was interested in her and her history and sweetly sympathetic concerning her woes and worries. To such a friend Ingua might confide anything, almost; and, while she was not fully aware of that fact just now, she said impulsively:

"Without tellin' what'd cost me my life, or lettin' anybody know what's become of Ned Joselyn, I'll say they was money—lots o' money!—passed atween him an' ol' Swaller-tail. Sometimes the heap went to one, an' sometimes to the other; I seen it with my own eyes, when Gran'dad didn't know I was spyin'. But it didn't stick to either one, for Ned was—" She stopped short, then continued more slowly: "When Ned dis'peared, he'd spent all his own an' his wife's money, an' Ol' Swallertail ain't got enough t' live decent."

"Are you sure of that, Ingua?"

"N-o, I ain't sure o' noth'n. But he don't spend no money, does he?"

"For stamps," Mary Louise reminded her.

Then the child grew silent and thoughtful again. Mary Louise, watching the changing expressions on her face, was convinced she knew more of the mystery than she dared confide to her new friend. There was no use trying to force her confidence, however; in her childish way she was both shrewd and stubborn and any such attempt would be doomed to failure. But after quite a period of silence Mary Louise asked gently:

"Did you like Mr. Joselyn, Ingua?"

"Sometimes. Only when—" Another self-interruption. She seemed often on the point of saying something her better judgment warned her not to. "Sometimes Ned were mighty good to me. Sometimes he brought me candy, when things was goin' good with him. Once, Mary Louise, he kissed me, an' never wiped off his mouth afterwards! Y-e-s, I liked Ned, 'ceptin' when—" Another break. "I thought Ned was a pretty decent gink."

"Where did you learn all your slang, dear?"

"What's slang?"

"Calling a man a 'gink,' and words like that." "Oh. Marm was full o' them words," she replied with an air of pride. "They seem to suit things better than common words; don't you think so, Mary Louise?"

"Sometimes," with an indulgent smile. "But ladies do not use them, Ingua, because they soil the purity of our language."

"Well," said the girl, "it'll be a long time, yit, afore I'm a lady, so I guess I'll talk like Marm did. Marm weren't a *real* lady, to my mind, though she claimed she'd show anybody that said she wasn't. Real ladies don't leave the'r kids in the clutches of Ol' Swallertails."

Mary Louise did not think it wise to criticize the unknown Mrs. Scammel or to allow the woman's small daughter to do so. So she changed the subject to more pleasant and interesting topics and the afternoon wore speedily away.

Finally Ingua jumped up and said:

"I gotta go. If Gran'dad don't find supper ready there'll be another rumpus, an' I've been so happy to-day that I want to keep things pleasant-like."

"Won't you take the rest of these cakes with you?" urged Mary Louise.

"Nope. I'll eat one more, on my way home, but I ain't one o' them tramps that wants food pushed at 'em in a bundle. We ain't got much to home, but what we got's ours."

A queer sort of mistaken pride, Mary Louise reflected, as she watched the girl spring lightly over the stepping-stones and run up the opposite bank. Evidently Ingua considered old Mr. Cragg her natural guardian and would accept nothing from others that he failed to provide her with. Yet, to judge from her speech, she detested her grandfather and regarded him with unspeakable aversion.

CHAPTER VII

MARY LOUISE CALLS FOR HELP

All the queer hints dropped by the girl that afternoon, concerning the relations between Mr. Joselyn and Mr. Cragg, were confided by Mary Louise to her Gran'pa Jim that evening, while the old Colonel listened with grave interest.

"I'm sure there is some mystery here," declared Mary Louise, "and maybe we are going to discover some dreadful crime."

"And, on the contrary," returned Colonel Hathaway, "the two men may have been interested together in some business venture that resulted disastrously and led Mr. Joselyn to run away to escape his wife's reproaches. I consider that a more logical solution of your mystery, my dear."

"In that case," was her quick reply, "why is Mr. Cragg still writing scores of letters and getting bags full of replies? I don't believe that business deal—whatever it was—is ended, by any means. I think that Ned Joselyn and Old Swallowtail are still carrying it on, one in hiding and the other here—and to be here is to be in hiding, also. And it isn't an honest business, Gran'pa Jim, or they wouldn't be so secret about it."

The Colonel regarded his young granddaughter with surprise.

"You seem quite logical in your reasoning, my dear," he confessed, "and, should your conjectures prove correct, these men are using the mails for illegal purposes, for which crime the law imposes a severe penalty. But consider, Mary Louise, is it our duty to trail criminals and through our investigations bring them to punishment?"

Mary Louise took time to consider this question, as she had been advised to do. When she replied she had settled the matter firmly in her mind.

"We are part of the Government, Gran'pa Jim," she asserted. "If we believe the Government is being wronged—which means the whole people is being wronged—I think we ought to uphold the law and bring the wrong-doer to justice."

"Allowing that," said her grandfather, "let us next consider what grounds you have for your belief that wrong is being committed. Are they not confined to mere suspicions? Suspicions aroused by the chatter of a wild, ungoverned child? Often the amateur detective gets into trouble through accusing the innocent. Law-abiding citizens should not attempt to uncover all the wrongs that exist, or to right them. The United States Government employs special officers for such duties."

Mary Louise was a bit nettled, failing to find at the moment any argument to refute this statement. She was still convinced, however, that the mystery was of grave importance and she believed it would be intensely exciting to try to solve it. Gran'pa Jim was not acquainted with Ingua Scammel and had not listened to the girl's unconscious exposures; so, naturally, he couldn't feel just as Mary Louise did about this matter. She tried to read, as her grandfather, considering the conversation closed, was now doing. They sat together by the lamplight in the cozy sitting room. But her thoughts constantly reverted to "Old Swallowtail" and to Ingua. At length she laid down her book and said:

"Gran'pa, would you mind if I invited Josie O'Gorman to come here and make me a visit?"

He gave her a curious look, which, soon melted into an amused smile.

"Not at all, my dear. I like Josie. But I can see by your desire to introduce a female detective on the scene that you cannot abandon your suspicion of Mr. Cragg."

"I want to save Ingua, if I can," replied the girl earnestly. "The poor little thing can't go on leading such a life without its ruining all her future, even if her grandfather's brutal threats are mere bluff. And Josie isn't a female detective, as yet; she is only training to be one, because her father has won fame in that profession."

"Josie O'Gorman," said the Colonel, meditatively, "is a wonderfully clever girl. I believe she is better, even now, than a score of average male sleuths. Perhaps it will be a desirable thing for her to come here, for she will be shrewd enough to decide, in a short time, whether or not your suspicions are justified. In the latter case, you will be relieved of your worries. Will you abide by Josie's decision?"

"Will you, Gran'pa Jim?"

"I have considerable confidence in the girl's judgment."

"Then I will write to her at once."

She went to her desk and wrote the following note:

Dear Josie: We are at the dropping-off-place of the world, a stagnant little village of a dozen houses set in an oasis that is surrounded by the desert of civilization. And here, where life scarcely throbs, I've scented a mystery that has powerfully impressed me and surely needs untangling. It will be good practice for you, Josie, and so I want you to pack up at once and come to us on a good long visit. We're delightfully situated and, even if the mystery dissolves into thin air under the sunshine of your eyes, I know you will enjoy the change and our dreamy, happy existence in the wilds of nowhere. Gran'pa Jim wants you, too, as he thinks your coming will do me good, and his judgment is never at fault. So drop me a postal to say when you will arrive and I will meet you at Chargrove Station with our car. Affectionately your friend, Mary Louise Burrows.

Gran'pa Jim read this note and approved it, so next morning Mary Louise walked to the village and deposited it in the postoffice, which located in the front room of Jim Bennett's little residence and was delightfully primitive. Jim was "jus' makin' up the mail bag," he said, so her letter was in time to catch the daily train and would be in Washington, where Josie lived, in the quickest possible time.

Josie O'Gorman was about the same age as Mary Louise and she was the only child of John O'Gorman, famed as one of the cleverest detectives in the Secret Service. Josie was supposed to have inherited some of her father's talent; at least her fond parent imagined so. After carefully training the child almost from babyhood, O'Gorman had tested Josie's ability on just one occasion, when she had amply justified her father's faith in her. This test had thrown the girl into association with Mary Louise and with Colonel Hathaway, both of whom greatly admired her cleverness, her clear head and shrewd judgment. Mary Louise, especially, had developed a friendship for the embryo girl detective and had longed to know her more intimately. So she congratulated herself on the happy thought of inviting Josie to Cragg's Crossing and was delighted that the vague mystery surrounding the Cragg family offered an adequate excuse to urge the girl to come to her. There seemed nothing in the way of such a visit, for Officer O'Gorman, however pleased he might be at his daughter's success in her first detective case, declared Josie yet too young to enter active service and insisted that she acquire further age and experience before he would allow her to enter her chosen profession in earnest. "One swallow," he said, "doesn't make a summer, and the next bird you fly might prove a buzzard, my dear. Take your time, let your wits mature, and you'll be the better for it in the end."

So Mary Louise waited impatiently for Josie's reply, meantime seeing as much of Ingua as she could and trying to cement the growing friendship between them. Ingua responded eagerly to her advances and as old Mr. Cragg was away from home the greater part of the day there was much crossing of the stepping-stones by both girls and more than one "afternoon tea" in the pavilion.

"Do you know," said Ingua one day, in confidential mood, "I haven't had the devils since that time I started to run away and you stopped me? P'r'aps it's because I'm not as hungry as I used to be; but, anyhow, I'm glad I stayed. Gran'dad's been good, too, 'though he's got the 'wakes' ag'in."

"What are the 'wakes'?" asked Mary Louise.

"Can't sleep nights. Goes t' bed on time, ye know, but gits up ag'in an' dresses himself an' walks."

"In the house?"

"No, walks out o' doors. Sometimes he'll come in at jes' daylight; sometimes not till break-fas' is ready."

"And doesn't that make him cross, Ingua?"

"Not a bit. It seems to chirk him up. Yist'day mornin', when he come in, he was feelin' so chipper he give me a cent, an' told me to buy somethin' useful. I guess that's the first cent he ever give me. I've *took* money o' his'n, but he never *give* me none afore."

"Oh, Ingua! I hope you haven't stolen money?"

"Nope. Jes' took it. It ain't easy, 'cause he knows ev'ry cent he's got, an' it ain't often he leaves it where I kin git it. P'r'aps he knows it's me, but when I lie out of it he can't do noth'n' but growl—an' growlin' don't hurt any."

Mary Louise was greatly distressed. This reckless disregard of property rights was of course the direct result of the child's environment, but must be corrected. Ingua resented direct chiding and it was necessary to point out to her the wickedness of stealing in the gentlest possible manner.

"How much money have you taken from your grandfather?" she asked.

"Oh, not much. A nickel, now an' then. He wouldn't stan' for losin' any more, ye see. P'r'aps, altogether, I've swiped twenty-five cents. But once Ned Joselyn give me a dollar, an' Ol' Swallertail knowed it, an' made me give it to him to save for me. That were the last I ever saw o' that dollar, Mary Louise, so I ain't even with Gran'dad yet."

"Do you think," remarked Mary Louise, "there is ever any excuse for stealing?"

Edith Van Dyne

The girl stared at her, coloring slightly.

"Do ye mean Gran'dad, er *me?*"

"I mean you. He didn't steal your dollar, dear; he merely took it so you wouldn't spend it foolishly."

"An' I merely took them nickels so's I could, spend 'em foolish. There's no fun in spendin' money, seems to me, unless you squander it reckless. That's what I done with them nickels. Candy an' chewin' gum tastes better when you know it's swiped."

Mary Louise sighed. It was so hard to show little Ingua the error of her ways.

"As fer stealin'—out an' out *stealin',*" continued the girl, with a proud toss of her head, "we Craggs ain't never took noth'n' that don't belong to us from nobody. What a Cragg takes from a Cragg is a Cragg's business, an' when we takes someth'n' from somebody else I'll ask ye to tell me 'bout it."

"Where are you going, Ingua?"

"Home."

"You're not offended, I hope."

"No, but I got work to do. I ain't done my breakfas' dishes yet."

Mary Louise musingly watched the girl cross the river. On the opposite bank she turned to wave her hand and then ran into the cottage. Ingua's code of honor was a peculiar one. Her pride in the Craggs seemed unaccountable, considering she and her grandfather were the only two of the family in existence—except that wandering mother of hers.

But the recent conversation had uncovered a new phase of the mystery. Old Swallowtail was nervous over something; he could not sleep at night, but roamed the roads while others with clear consciences slumbered. There must be some powerful reason to account for the old man's deserting his bed in this manner. What could it be?

When she walked over to the postoffice the girl found the long-looked-for letter from Josie O'Gorman. It said:

Dear Mary Louise: How good you are! I positively need a change of scene and a rest, so I'm coming. To-morrow—by the train to Chargrove. The mystery you hint at will help me to rest. Dad doesn't want me to grow rusty and he has some odd theories I'd like to work out. I haven't an idea what your "mystery" is, of course, but if it enables me to test any one of the O'Gorman theories (a theory is merely a stepping-stone to positive information) I shall bless you forever. And that reminds me: I'm coming as a sewing girl, to help you fix over some summer gowns. You're anxious to give me the work, because I need it, but as we're rather chummy I'm half servant and half companion. (I hate sewing and make the longest stitches you ever saw!) Moreover, I'm Josie Jessup. I'm never an O'Gorman while I'm working on a mystery; it wouldn't do at all. Explain this to dear old Gran'pa Jim.

Between the receipt of this script and to-morrow's train jot down in regular order everything you know concerning the aforesaid mystery. Make it brief; no speculations or suspicions, just facts. Then I won't waste any time getting busy.

Can you hear the rumble of my train? While you're reading this I'm on my way!

Josie

Edith Van Dyne

"Good!" murmured Mary Louise, as she folded the letter. "I feel better already. Whatever the mystery of Old Swallowtail may be, Josie is sure to solve it."

CHAPTER VIII

THE RED-HEADED GIRL

Sol Jerrems the storekeeper, coming in from the back room where he had been drawing molasses for Farmer Higgins, found perched on top the sugar-barrel a chunky, red-haired, freckle-faced young girl whom he had never seen before. She seemed perfectly at home in his store and sat with her knees drawn up to her chin and her arms encircling her legs, eyeing soberly the two or three farmers who had come to the Crossing to "trade."

"If the head o' thet bar'l busts in, you'll be a fine mess," remarked Sol.

The girl nodded but did not move from her position. Sol waited on his customers, at times eyeing the strange girl curiously. When the farmers had gone with their purchases he approached the barrel and examined his visitor with speculative care.

"Want anything?"

"Spool o' red cotton, number thirty."

"Ain't got no red."

"Green'll do."

"Ain't got green. Only black an' white."

"All right."

"Want black or white?"

"No."

Sol leaned against the counter. He wasn't busy; the girl seemed in no hurry; it was a good time to gossip and find out all about the strange creature perched on his sugar-barrel.

"Where'd ye come from?" he inquired.

"City," tossing her head toward the north.

"What for?"

"To do sewing for the Hathaways folks. Mary Louise, you know."

Sol pricked up his ears. The Hathaways were newcomers, about whom little was known. He wanted to know more, and here was a girl who could give him inside information.

"Knowed the Hathaways in the city?"

"Kind o'. Sewed on Mary Louise's spring dresses. How long you been here?"

"Me? Why, I come here more'n twenty years ago. What does the Colonel do in the city?"

"Never asked him. Why do they call this place

Cragg's Crossing?"

"I didn't name it. S'pose 'cause ol' Cragg used to own all the land, an' the roads crossed in the middle o' his farm."

"What Cragg was that?"

"Eh? Why, father to Ol' Swallertail. Ever seen Ol' Swallertail?"

"No."

"Wal, he's a sight fer sore eyes. First time anybody sees him they either laughs er chokes. The movin'-pictur' folks would go crazy over him. Ever seen a movin'-pictur'?"

"Yes."

"I did, too, when I was in the city las' year. Ol' Swallertail 'minds me of 'em. Goes 'round dressed up like George Washington when he crossed the Delaware."

"Crazy?"

"That way, yes; other ways, not a bit. Pretty foxy gent, is Ol' Swallertail."

"Why?"

Sol hesitated, reflecting. These questions were natural, in a stranger, but to explain old Hezekiah Cragg's character was not a particularly easy task.

"In the fust place, he drives a hard bargain. Don't spend money, but allus has it. Keeps busy, but keeps his business to himself."

Edith Van Dyne

"What is his business?"

"Didn't I say he kep' it to himself?"

"But he owns all the land around here."

"Not now. He owns jest a half-acre, so far's anybody knows, with a little ol' hut on it thet a respect'ble pig wouldn't live in. It's jes' acrost the river from the place where you're workin'."

"Then what has become of his land?"

"It's stayed jes' where it allus was, I guess," with a chuckle at his own wit, "but Ol' Swaller-tail sold it, long ago. Ol' Nick Cragg, his father afore him, sold a lot of it, they say, and when he died he left half his ready money an' all his land to Hezekiah—thet's Ol' Swallertail—an' the other half o' his money to his second son, Peter."

"Where is Peter?" asked the girl quickly.

"Went back to Ireland, years ago, and never's be'n heard of since. The Craggs was Irish afore they got to be Americans, but it seems Pete hankered fer th' Ol' Sod an' quit this country cold."

"So the Craggs are Irish, eh?" mused the girl in a casual tone. And then she yawned, as if not greatly interested. But Sol was interested, so long as he was encouraged to talk.

"I be'n told, by some o' the ol' settlers," he went on, "thet ol' Nick Cragg were born in Ireland, was a policeman in New York—where he made his first money—an' then come here an' bought land an' settled down. They ain't much difference 'tween a policeman an' a farmer, I guess. If the story's true, it proves Ol' Swallertail has Irish blood in him yit, though fer that matter he's lived here long enough to be jes' American, like the rest of us. After he come inter the property he gradual-like sold off all the land, piece by piece, till he ain't got noth'n left but thet half-acre. Sold most of it afore I come here, an' I be'n at the Crossing more'n twenty year."

"If the land brought a fair price, Old Swallowtail ought to be rich," remarked the girl.

"Then he ain't what he orter be. Folks says he specilated, years ago, an' got stung. I know him pretty well—as well as anybody knows him—an' my opinion is he ain't got more'n enough to bury him decent."

"Thought you said he drives a hard bargain?"

"Young woman," said Sol earnestly, "the man don't live as kin make money specilatin'. The game's ag'in him, fust an' last, an' the more brains he's got the harder he'll git stung."

"But I thought you said Mr. Cragg has a business."

"An' I said nobody knows what it is. When Ned Joselyn used to come here the two was thick, an' Ned were a specilater through an' through. Some thinks it was him as got Cragg's wad, an' some says he lost it all, an' his wife's money, too. Anyhow, Joselyn lit out fer good an' when he were gone Ann Kenton cried like a baby an' ol' Swallertail 's been dumb as a clam ever since."

"What makes you think Cragg has a business?" persisted the girl.

"He keeps an office, over the store here, an' he has a sign on the door thet says 'Real Estate.' But he ain't got no real estate, so that ain't why he shuts himself in the office day after

Edith Van Dyne

day—an' even Sundays. He's got some other business. Ev'ry night, afore he goes home, he takes a bunch o' letters to Mrs. Bennett's postoffice, an' ev'ry mornin' he goes there an' gits another bunch o' letters that's come to him in the mail. If that don't mean some sort o' business, I don't know what'n thunder it *does* mean."

"Nor I," said the girl, yawning again. "What about Ned Joselyn? Was he nice?"

"Dressed like a dandy, looked like a fool, acted like the Emp'ror o' Rooshy an' pleased ev'rybody by runnin' away. That is, ev'rybody but his wife an' Ol' Swallertail."

"I see. Who else lives over your store?"

"I live there myself; me an' my fambly, in the back part. One o' the front rooms I rents to Ol' Swallertail, an' he pays the rent reg'lar. The other front room Miss Huckins, the dressmaker, lives in."

"Oh. I'm a dressmaker, too. Guess I'll go up and see her. Is she in?"

"When she's out, she leaves the key with me, an' the key ain't here. Say, girl, what's yer name?"

"Josie."

"Josie what?"

"Jessup. Pa was a drayman. Ever hear of him?"

"No. But about the Hathaways; what has—"

"And you've got no red thread? Or green?"

"Only black an' white. Does the Colonel—"

"Can't use black or white," said the girl, deliberately getting off the barrel. "Guess I'll go up and ask Miss Huckins if she has any red."

Out she walked, and old Sol rubbed his wrinkled forehead with a bewildered look and muttered:

"Drat the gal! She's pumped me dry an' didn't tell me a word about them Hathaway folks. She worse'n ol' Eben, the nigger help. Seems like nobody wants t' talk about the Hathaways, an' that means there's somethin' queer about 'em. But this red-headed sewin'-girl is a perfec' innercent an' I'll git her talkin' yet, if she stays here long."

Meantime Josie mounted the stairs, which were boarded in at one end of the building, being built on the outside to economize space, and entered the narrow upper hallway. A chatter of children's voices in the rear proclaimed that portion to be the quarters of the Jerrems family. Toward the front was a door on which, in dim letters, was the legend: "H. Cragg. Real Estate."

Here the girl paused to listen. No sound came from the interior of H. Cragg's apartment. Farther along she found a similar door on which was a card reading: "Miss Huckins, Dressmaker and Milliner." Listening again, she heard the sound of a flatiron thumping an ironing board.

She knocked, and the door was opened by a little middle-aged woman who held a hot flatiron in one hand. She was thin; she was bright-eyed; her hair was elaborately dressed with little ringlets across the forehead and around the ears, so Josie at once decided it was a wig.

Seeing a stranger before her, Miss Huckins looked her over carefully from head to foot, while Josie smiled a vacuous, inconsequent smile and said in a perfunctory way:

"Good morning."

"Come in," returned Miss Huckins, with affable civility. "I don't think I know you."

"I'm Josie Jessup, from the city. I'm in your line, Miss Huckins—in a way, that is. I've come here to do some sewing for Mary Louise Burrows, who is the granddaughter of Colonel Hathaway, who has rented the Kenton Place. Nice weather, isn't it?"

Miss Huckins was not enthusiastic. Her face fell. She had encouraged sundry hopes that the rich little girl would employ her to do whatever sewing she might need. So she resumed the pressing of a new dress that was spread over her ironing-board and said rather shortly:

"Anything I can do for you?"

"I want to use some red thread and the storekeeper doesn't keep it in stock. Queer old man, that storekeeper, isn't he?"

"I don't call him queer. He's honest as the day is long and makes a good landlord. Country stores don't usually keep red thread, for it is seldom used."

"He has been talking to me about old Mr. Cragg, who has an office next door to you. I'm sure you'll admit that Mr. Cragg is queer, if the storekeeper isn't."

"A man like Mr. Cragg has the right to be queer," snapped the dressmaker, who did not relish this criticism of the natives by a perfect stranger. "He is very quiet and respectable and makes a very satisfactory neighbor."

Josie, seated in a straight, wood-bottomed chair, seemed not at all chagrined by her reception. She watched the pressing for a time silently.

"That's a mighty pretty gown," she presently remarked, in a tone of admiration. "I don't suppose I shall ever be able to make anything as nice as that. I—I'm not good at planning, you know," with modest self-deprecation. "I only do plain sewing and mending."

The stern features of Miss Huckins relaxed a bit. She glanced at the girl, then at her work, and said more pleasantly than she had before spoken:

"This dress is for Mary Donovan, who lives two miles north of here. She's to be married next Saturday—if they get the haying over with by that time—and this is part of her trousseau. I've made her two other dresses and trimmed two hats for her—a straw shape and a felt Gainsboro. The Donovans are pretty well-to-do."

Josie nodded with appreciation.

"It's nice she can get such elegant things so near home, isn't it? Why, she couldn't do as well in the city—not *half* as well!"

Miss Huckins held up the gown and gazed at it with unmistakable pride. "It's the best Henrietta," said she, "and I'm to get six dollars for the making. I wanted seven, at first, and Mary only wanted to pay five, so we split the difference. With all the other things, I didn't do so badly on this trousseau."

"You're in luck," declared Josie, "and so is Mary Donovan. Doesn't Mr. Cragg do any business except real estate?"

"I think he must," replied the dressmaker, hanging up the gown and then seating herself opposite her visitor. "All the real estate business he's done in the last two years was to rent the Kenton Place to Colonel Hathaway and make a sale of Higgins' cow pasture to Sam Marvin. But he's so quiet, all day, in the next room, that I can't figure out what he's up to. No one goes near him, so I can't overhear any talk. One time, of course, Mr. Joselyn used to go there, and then they always whispered, as if they were up to some deviltry. But after the quarrel Joselyn never came here again."

"Oh, did they quarrel?" asked Josie, with languid interest. She knew her praise of the dress had won the dressmaker's heart and also she was delighted to find Miss Huckins a more confirmed and eager gossip than even Sol Jerrems.

"I should say they did quarrel!" was the emphatic reply, although she sank her voice to a whisper and glanced warningly at the thin partition. "At one time I thought there'd be murder done, for Joselyn yelled: 'Take that away—take it away!' and Old Swallowtail—that's the name we call Mr. Cragg, you know—roared out: 'You deserve to die for this cowardly act.' Well, you'd better believe my hair stood on end for a minute," Josie smiled as she thought of the wig standing on end, "but nothing happened. There was deep silence. Then the door opened and Mr. Joselyn walked out. I never interfere with other people's business, but attend strictly to my own, yet that day I was so flustered that I peeked through a crack of my door at Mr. Joselyn and he seemed cool as a cucumber. Then Mr. Cragg slammed the door of his room—which is z very unusual thing for him to do—and that was all."

"When did this happen?" asked Josie.

"Last fall, just before Mrs. Joselyn and her husband went back to their city home. Some time in the winter Mr. Joselyn ran away from her, they say, but I guess old Cragg had nothing do with that. Around here, Joselyn wasn't liked. He put on too many airs of superiority to please the country folks. Sol Jerrems thinks he made away with Mr. Cragg's money, in unwise speculations, but I don't believe Cragg had any money to lose. He seems as poor as I am."

"What do you suppose drew those two men together, Miss Huckins?" inquired the girl.

"I can't say. I've tried to figure it out, but the truth is that old Cragg don't confide in anyone—not even in me, and we're close neighbors. You couldn't find two men in all America more different than Joselyn and Cragg, and yet they had dealings of some sort together and were friendly, for a time."

Josie sighed regretfully.

"I like to hear about these mysterious things," said she. "It's almost as good as reading a story. Only, in this case, we will never know how the story ends."

"Well, perhaps not," admitted the dressmaker. "Joselyn is gone and no one'll ever get the truth out of Cragg. But—I'd like to know, myself, not only how the story ends but what it was all about. Just now all we know is that there *was* a story, of some sort or other, and perhaps is yet."

A period of silence, while both mused.

"I don't suppose you could find a bit of red thread?" said Josie.

Edith Van Dyne

"No, I haven't used it for ages. Is it to mend with?"

"Yes."

"If it's a red dress, use black thread. It won't show, if you're careful; and it won't fade away and leave a white streak, like red sometimes does."

"Thank you, Miss Huckins." She rose to go. "I'd like to drop in again, sometime, for a little visit."

"Come as often as you like," was the cordial reply.

"Cragg's Crossing people are rather interesting; they're so different from city folks," said Josie.

"Yes, they really are, and I know most of them pretty well. Come in again, Josie."

"Thank you; I will."

CHAPTER IX

JOSIE INVESTIGATES

"Well, what luck?" asked Mary Louise, as she came into Josie's room while her friend was dressing for dinner.

"Not much," was the reply. "I'm not at all sure, Mary Louise, that this chase will amount to anything. But it will afford me practice in judging human nature, if nothing else comes of it, so I'm not at all sorry you put me on the trail. When are we to see Ingua again?"

"To-morrow afternoon. She's coming to tea in the pavilion."

"That's good. Let me see all of her you can. She's an original, that child, and I'm going to like her. Our natures are a good deal alike."

"Oh, Josie!"

"That's a fact. We're both proud, resentful, reckless and affectionate. We hate our enemies and love our friends. We're rebellious, at times, and not afraid to defy the world."

"I'm sure you are not like that, dear," protested Mary Louise.

Edith Van Dyne

"I am. Ingua and I are both children of nature. The only difference is that I am older and have been taught diplomacy and self-control, which she still lacks. I mask my feelings, while Ingua frankly displays hers. That's why I am attracted to her."

Mary Louise did not know how to combat this mood. She remained silent until Josie was dressed and the two went down to dinner. Their visitor was no longer the type of a half ignorant, half shrewd sewing-girl, such as she had appeared to be while in the village. Her auburn hair was now tastefully arranged and her attire modest and neat. She talked entertainingly during dinner, enlivening her companions thereby, and afterward played a game of dominoes with the Colonel in the living-room, permitting him to beat her at this, his favorite diversion.

Both the old gentleman and his granddaughter enjoyed their evenings with Josie O'Gorman, for she proved delightful company. In the mornings, however, she would don her cheap gingham, rumple her hair, and pose throughout the day as Josie Jessup the sewing-girl.

Ingua, at first shy of the visitor, soon developed a strong liking for Josie and would talk with her more freely than with Mary Louise. Josie would skip across the stepping-stones and help Ingua wash the breakfast dishes and sweep the bare little rooms of the cottage and then together they would feed the chickens, gather the eggs and attend to such daily tasks as Ingua was obliged to fulfill. With Josie's help this was soon accomplished and then the child was free for the day and could run across to join Mary Louise, while Josie sallied to the village to interview the natives.

When the girl detective had been at Cragg's Crossing for a week she was a familiar figure to the villagers—every one of whom was an acquaintance—and had gleaned all the information it was possible to secure from them, which was small in amount and unsatisfactory in quality. Two or three times she had passed Old Swallowtail on the street, but he had not seemed to notice her. Always the old man stared straight ahead, walking stiffly and with a certain repellent dignity that forbade his neighbors to address him. He seemed to see no one. He lived in a world known only to himself and neither demanded nor desired association with his fellows.

"An eccentric; bigoted, sullen and conceited," reflected Josie, in considering his character. "Capable of any cruelty or crime, but too cautious to render himself liable to legal punishment. The chances are that such a man would never do any great wrong, from cowardly motives. He might starve and threaten a child, indeed, but would refrain from injuring one able to resent the act. Nevertheless, he quarreled with Joselyn—and Joselyn disappeared. There was some reason for that quarrel; some reason for that disappearance; some reason why a man like Edward Joselyn made Old Swallowtail his confidential friend. A business connection, perhaps. Before daring a conjecture I must discover what business Cragg is engaged in."

She soon discovered that Ingua was as ignorant of her grandfather's business life as were all others. One day, as the two girls were crossing the stepping-stones to reach the pavilion, after "doing" the morning housework, Josie remarked:

"In winter one could cross here on the ice."

"Oh, no," replied Ingua, "the water don't freeze. It runs too fast. But sometimes it gits over the top o' the stones, an' then you has to step keerful to keep from fallin' in."

"Did you ever try to cross at such a time?" "Once I did, an' I was skeered, you kin bet. But I says to myself: 'If Ol' Swallertail kin make the crossin', I kin—dark or no dark—an' by cracky I tackled it brave as a lion."

"You tried to cross in the dark, on a winter's night? What for, Ingua?"

Ingua, walking beside her up the bank, paused with a startled expression and grew red. Her eyes, narrowed and shrewd, fixed themselves suspiciously on Josie's face. But the other returned the look with a bland smile that surely ought to disarm one more sophisticated than this simple child.

"I mustn't talk 'bout that," said Ingua in a low voice. "Jes' fergit as I said it, Josie."

"Why?"

"Do ye want me choked, or killed?"

"Who would do that?"

"Gran'dad would, if I blabbed."

"Shucks!"

"Ye don't know Gran'dad—not when he's got the temper on him. If ye'd seen what I seen, ye'd know that he'd keep his word—'to, kill me if I talk too much."

Josie sat down on top the bank.

"What did you see, Ingua?"

"Ye'll hev to guess it."

"It looks that way," said Josie calmly; "but you needn't be afraid of *me,* Ingua. You and I could know a lot of things, together, and keep 'em to ourselves. Don't you think I'm a good enough friend not to get you choked or killed by telling any secrets you confided to me? And—look here, Ingua— this secret is worrying you a good deal."

"Who says so?"

"I do. You'd feel a heap better if you told me about it, for then we could talk it over together when we're alone."

Ingua sat down beside her, gazing thoughtfully at the river.

"You'd tell Mary Louise."

"You know better than that. A secret's a secret, isn't it? I guess I can keep my mouth shut when I want to, Ingua."

Josie had a way of imitating Ingua's mode of speech when they were together. It rendered their intercourse more free and friendly. But the girl did not reply at once. She sat dreamily reflecting upon the proposition and its possible consequences. Finally she said in a hesitating way:

"I wisht I knew what ter do. I sometimes think I orter tell somebody that knows more'n I do, Josie, if I ever blab at all."

"Try me, Ingua. I'm pretty smart, 'cause I've seen more of the big world than you have, and know what goes on in the big, busy cities, Where life is different from what it is in this little place. I've lived in more than one city, too, and that means a lot of experience for a girl of my age. I'm sure I could help you, dear. Perhaps, when I've heard your story, I will tell you never to say anything about it to anyone else; and then, on the other hand, I might think differently. Anyhow, I'd never tell, myself, any secret of yours, whatever I might think, because I'd cut off my right hand rather than get you into trouble."

This dramatic speech was intended to appeal to the child's imagination and win her full confidence. In a way, it succeeded. Ingua sidled closer to Josie and finally said in a trembling whisper:

"Ye wouldn't git Gran'dad inter trouble either, would ye?"

"Do you like him, Ingua?"

"I hate him! But he's a Cragg, an' I'm a Cragg, an' the Craggs kin stand up an' spit at the world, if they wants to."

"That's right," agreed Josie, emphatically. "We've got to stick up for our own families and fight for our good name when it's necessary. Do you think I'd let anybody get the best of a Jessup? Never in a thousand years!"

Ingua nodded her head as if pleased.

"That's the way I look at it, Josie. Ev'rybody's down on Ol' Swallertail, an' I'm down on him myself, fer that matter; but I'll dare anybody to say anything ag'in him when I'm aroun'. An' yet, Josie—an' yet—I ain't sure but he's—but he's a *murderer!*"

She had dropped her voice until she scarcely breathed the last words and her little body trembled through and through with tense nervousness. Josie took her hand.

"Never mind, dear," she said gently. "Perhaps he didn't kill Ned Joselyn, after all."

Ingua sprang up with a hoarse scream and glared at Josie in absolute terror.

"How'd ye know? How'd ye know it were Ned Joselyn?" she demanded, trembling more and more.

Josie's reply was a smile. Josie's smile was essentially winning and sweet. It was reassuring, trustful, friendly.

"This isn't a very big place, Ingua," she quietly remarked. "I can count the people of Cragg's Crossing on my fingers and toes, and the only one who has ever disappeared is Ned Joselyn. Why, you've told me so yourself. Your grandfather and Joselyn were friends. Then they quarreled. Afterward Joselyn disappeared."

"Who said they quarreled?"

"Miss Huckins told me. It was in the office, next door to where she lives and works."

"Oh," with a sigh of relief. "But Ned Joselyn run away. Ev'rybody knows that."

"Everybody but you, dear. Sit down. Why do you get so nervous? Really, Ingua, after you've told me the whole story you'll feel better. It's too big a secret for one small body to hold, isn't it? And just between ourselves we will talk it all over—many times—and then it won't seem so dreadful to you. And, after all, you're not positive your grandfather killed Ned Joselyn. Perhaps he didn't. But you're afraid he did, and that keeps you unstrung and unhappy. Who knows but I may be able to help you discover the truth? Sit down, Ingua, and let's talk it all over."

CHAPTER X

INGUA IS CONFIDENTIAL

Ingua slowly resumed her seat on the bank beside her friend. It was hard to resist Josie's appeals.

"The whole thing looks pretty black ag'in Gran'dad," she said. "I s'pose ye can't understand what I mean till I tell ye the whole story, from the beginning 'cause ye didn't live here at the time. If ye lived here," she added, "I wouldn't tell ye anything, but by-'n'-by yer goin' away. An' ye've promised to keep yer mouth shut."

"Unless you give me permission to speak."

"I ain't likely to do that. I'm tellin' ye this, Josie, so's we kin talk it over, at times. It has got hold o' my mind, somethin' terrible. Once I was goin' to tell Mary Louise, but—she couldn't understand it like you kin. She's—diff'rent. And if Gran'dad ever hears that I blabbed I'm as good as dead, an' I know it!"

"He won't hear it from me," promised Josie.

"Well, Gran'dad was allus sly. I 'member Marm tellin' him to his face he were cold as ice an' sly as sin. Mann had a way o' sayin' what she thought o' him, an' he'd jes' look at her steady an' say nuth'n back. She was allus tryin' to git money out o' him, Marm was, an' when he said he didn't hev no money she tol' him she knew he did. She ransacked the whole house— an' even tore up the floor-boards—tryin' to find where he'd hid it. Her idee was that if he'd sold his land for a lot o' money, an' hadn't spent a cent, he must hev it yit. But I guess Marm didn't find no money, an' so she lit out. The day she lit out she said to him that he was too slick for her, but she could take care o' herself. All she wanted was for him to take care o' me. Gran'dad said he would; an' so he did. He didn't take any too much care o' me, an' I'd ruther he wouldn't. If I had more to eat, I wouldn't kick, but since Mary Louise come here an' invited me to tea so often I hain't be'n hungry a bit."

"Mary Louise likes company," said Josie. "Go on, dear."

"Well, after Ann Kenton got married, her new husban' come here, which was Ned Joselyn. I never took a fancy to Ann. She wasn't 'specially uppish, but she wasn't noth'n else, either. Ned made me laugh when I first seen him. He had one spectacle in one eye, with a string to ketch it if it fell off. He had striped clothes an' shiny shoes an' he walked as keerful as if he was afraid the groun' would git the bottoms o' them nice shoes dirty. He used to set in that summer-house an' smoke cigarettes an' read books. One day he noticed Ol' Swallertail, an' looked so hard at him that his one-eyed spectacle fell off a dozen times.

"That night he sent a letter to Gran'dad an' Gran'dad read it an' tore it up an' told the man that brung it there was no answer. That's all I knew till one night they come walkin' home together, chummy as a team o' mules. When they come to the bridge they shook hands an' Ol' Swallertail come to the house with a grin on his face—the first an' last grin I ever seen him have."

Edith Van Dyne

"Doesn't he ever laugh?" asked Josie.

"If he does, he laughs when no one is lookin'. But after that day I seen Ned Joselyn with Gran'dad a good deal. Sometimes he'd come to our house an' wait fer Ol' Swallertail to come home, an' they'd send me away an' tell me not to come back till I was called. That made me mighty curious to see what they was up to, so one day I crep' up behind the house an' peeked in the winder. They wasn't in the kitchen, so I went aroun' an' peeked through the winder o' Gran'dad's room, an' there they both sot, an' Gran'dad was countin' out money on the table. It must 'a' be'n gold money, 'cause it was yaller an' bigger ner cents er nickels. Ned put it all in his pocket, an' writ somethin' on a paper that Gran'dad put inter his big pocketbook. Then they both got up an' I made a run fer it an' hid behind the barn."

"When did that happen?" asked Josie.

"The first summer Ann was married. That was three summers ago, countin' this one. I was only a kid, then," said Ingua, as if realizing she was now two years older.

"And after that?" said Josie.

"Las' summer it was jes' the same. The two was thicker'n gumdrops, only Ned didn't go to the office no more. He allus came to our house instid. One day, when he was waitin' fer Ol' Swallertail, he says to me: 'Ingua, how'd ye like to be rollin' in money, an' live in a big city, an' hev yer own automobile to ride in, an' dress like a queen?'"

"'I'd like it,' says I.

"'Well,' says he,' it's boun' to happen, if Ol' Swallertail sticks to me an' does what I say. He's got the capital,' says Ned, 'an'

I got the brains; an' atween the two of us, Ingua,' says Ned, 'we'll corral half the money there is in America.'"

"'Will he stick?' says I."

"'I dunno,' says Ned. 'He's got queer ideas 'bout duty an' honesty that ain't pop'lar these days in business. But I'm gitt'n so now thet I kin lead him by the nose, an' I'll force him to waller in money afore I've done with him.'"

"'I don't see how that'll make me rollin' in money, anyhow,' I told him."

"'The ol' man'll die, pretty soon,' says Ned, 'an' then you'll git the money I make for him. By the time yer growed up, if not afore,' says he, 'you may be the riches' girl in the world. It all depends on how I kin bend that ol' stick of a gran'dad o' yourn.'"

"That was the day he gimme the dollar, an' Gran'dad come in in time to see it, an' took it away from me. It didn't set me up any, that talk o' Ned's, 'cause I didn't believe in them brains he bragged on, or his bein' able to lead Ol' Swallertail by the nose. Gran'dad begun gittin' kind o' harsh with Ned, afore the summer was over, which showed he wasn't bendin' much, and at the last—just afore Ned went away—the big quarrel come off. It wasn't the quarrel Miss Huckins knows about, but it happened right here. They'd sent me away from the house, like they always did, and I were layin' in the clover in the back yard, when there was a crash an' a yell. I jumped up an' run to the door, an' the table was tipped over an' a lot o' papers an' money scattered on the floor, an' behind the table stood Ol' Swallertail, white an' still, an' Ned point'n' a gun at him."

"What sort of a gun?" questioned Josie.

"One o' them hip-pocket sort. Same as Jim Bennett the mailman carries. Only Jim's ain't never loaded, 'cause he's afraid of it. I ain't sure Ned's was loaded, either, for when he seen me in the doorway he jes' slipped it in his pocket.

"' Very well,' says Gran'dad, 'I knows now what sort o' a man you are, Ned Joselyn.' An' Ned he answers back: 'An' I know what sort o' a man *you* are, ol' Cragg. Yer a hypercrit through an' through; ye preach squareness while yer as crooked as a snake, an' as p'isonous an' deadly, an' ye'd ruin yer bes' friend jes' to git a copper cent the best o' him.'"

"Gran'dad leaned over an' set the table on its legs ag'in. An' then he says slow an' cold: 'But I hain't offered to murder you; *not yet,* Ned Joselyn!'"

"Ned looked at him an' kinder shivered. An' Gran'dad said: 'Pick up them papers an' things, Ingua.'

"So I picked 'em up an' put 'em on the table an' they sent me away ag'in. I laid in the clover a whole hour, feelin' pretty nervous an' rocky, fer I didn't know what was goin' to happen. Noth'n' did happen, though, 'cept that Ned crossed the river on the steppin'-stones an' halfway over he turned an' laughed an' waved his hand at Gran'dad, who stood in the door an' watched him go. But Gran'dad didn't laugh. He says to me when I come in:

"'Ingua, if ever I'm found dead, you go to Dud Berkey, the constable, an' tell him to arrest Ned Joselyn for murder. D'ye understan'?'"

"'I sure do,' says I. 'Guess he'd 'a' shot ye, Gran'dad, if I hadn't come in just when I did.'"

"'An' see here,' he went on, 'unless I'm foun' dead, you keep mum 'bout what ye seen to-day. If ye blab a word to anyone, ye'll git me in trouble, an' I'll crush ye as willin' as I'd swat a fly. Me an' Ned is friends ag'in,' says he, 'but I don't trust him.'"

"'Does he trust you?' I asked him; an' at first he jus' looked at me an' scowled; but after a minute he answered: 'I don't know how wise the man is. P'r'aps he isn't a fool; but even wise men is foolish sometimes.'"

"Well, Josie, that was all, just then. Ned went with his wife Ann to the city, nex' day, an' things here went on as usual. Only, Gran'dad begun to git wakeful nights, an' couldn't sleep. He'd git up an' dress an' go outdoors an' walk aroun' till mornin'. He didn't say noth'n' to *me* about it, but I watched him, an' one mornin' when he come in I says: 'Why don't ye git some medicine o' Doc Jenkins to make ye sleep?' Then he busts out an' grabs me by the throat an' near choked the life out or me."

"'Ye spy—ye dirty little spy!' says he, 'ye keep yer eyes shut an' yer mouth shut, or I'll skin-ye alive!' says he."

"The way he looked at me, I was skeered stiff, an' I never said noth'n' more 'bout his sleepin' nights. I guess what made him mad was my sayin' he orter hev a doctor, 'cause doctors cost money an' Gran'dad's so poor he hates t' spend money unnecessary."

"Did he ever again try to choke you?"

"He tried once more, but I was too spry for him. It was a winter night, when it was cold in his room an' he come inter the kitchen, where there was a fire, to write. I sot behind the stove, tryin' to keep warm, an' after a time I seen him look up an' glare at the bare wall a long time. By-'n'-by he says in a low voice: 'Fer the Cause!' an' starts writin' ag'in. 'What cause are ye talkin' about, Gran'dad?' says I.

"I guess he'd fergot I was there, but now he gives a yell an' jumps up an' comes for me with his fingers twistin' and workin' like I'd seen 'em afore. I didn't wait fer him to git near me, you kin bet; I made a dive out the back door an' stood aroun' in the cold tryin' to keep warm while I give him time to cool off where the fire was. When he was writin' ag'in I sneaked in an' he didn't notice me. When Marm was here she used to josh him about the 'Cause,' an' once I heard her tell him she guessed the Cause was hoardin' his money so's to starve his family. Marm wasn't afraid of him, but I am, so I never whisper the word 'Cause' while he's around."

Josie sat in silent reflection for a time. Then she asked softly:

"Does he still walk at night, Ingua?"

"Sometimes. Not so much as he once did, though. He seems to take streaks o' bein' wakeful," explained the girl.

"Have you ever seen him come out, or go in?"

"Lots o' times. When it's moonlight I kin see him through my window, an' he can't see me 'cause my room is dark."

"And does he carry anything with him?"

"Not a thing. He jes' goes out like he does daytimes, an' comes back the same way."

Josie nodded her tousled red head, as if the answers pleased her.

"He's a very clever man, your grandfather," she remarked.

"He can fool not only his neighbors, but his own family. But you've more to tell me, Ingua."

"How d'ye know, Josie?"

"Because all this is just the beginning. It is something else that has been worrying you, dear."

Edith Van Dyne

CHAPTER XI

THE FATE OF NED JOSELYN

The child stared dreamily at the rushing water for several minutes. Then she looked earnestly into Josie's face. Finally, with a sigh, she said:

"I may as well go on an' finish it, I s'pose."

"To be sure," said Josie. "You haven't told me anything very important yet."

"The important part's comin'," asserted Ingua, her tone gradually assuming its former animation. "'Twas last winter on the Thursday between Christmas an' New Year's. It was cold an' snowin' hard, an' it gits dark early them days. Gran'dad an' me was eat'n' supper by lamplight when there come a knock at the door. I jumped up an' opened it an' there stood Ned Joselyn, in a big heavy coat that was loaded with snow, an' kid gloves on, an' his one-eyed spectacle on his face. He come in an' stood while I shut the door, an' Gran'dad glared at him like he does when the devils gits him, and said: 'What—more?'

"'Sure thing,' says Ned. 'Noth'n' lasts forever.'"

"'That's true,' says Gran'dad, holdin' himself in. Then he looks at me, an' back to Ned, an' says: 'I can't see ye here. Where ye stoppin'? At the Kenton house?'"

"'Jes' fer to-night,' says Ned. 'It's more private than a hotel.'"

"'Go home, then,' says Gran'dad. 'I'll come over, by-'n'-by.'"

"Ned opened the door an' went out, sayin' noth'n' more. Gran'dad finished his supper an' then sot by the stove an' smoked his pipe while I washed the dishes. I wondered why he didn't go over an' see Ned, but he sot there an' smoked till I went upstairs to bed. That was queer, for I never knew him to smoke more'n one pipe o' tobacco at a time, before, an' then mostly on Sundays. And I'd never seen his face so hard an' cruel-lookin' as it were that night, and his eyes, seemed like they were made of glass. I didn't undress, fer I knowed there'd be trouble if he went over to Ned's house, and I made up my mind to keep watch o' things.

"So I set still in my room in the attic, an' Gran'dad set still in the room downstairs, an' it must 'a' be'n pretty late when I heard him get up an' go out. I slipped down right after him, meanin' to foller him, an' let myself out the back door so's he wouldn't see me. It had stopped snowin' by then, but it was so cold that the air cut like a knife and the only jacket I had wasn't any too warm fer such weather.

"When I got 'round the house Ol' Swallertail was standin' on the bank, lookin' at the river. I never knew nobody to try the steppin'-stones in winter, an' I s'posed o' course Gran'dad would take the path to the bridge; but he went down the bank, wadin' through the snow, an' started to cross over. The moon an' the snow made it light enough to see easy, after you'd be'n out a few minutes. I watched him cross over an' climb the bank an' make for the house, an' then I run down to the river myself.

"The water covered all the stones, but I knew where they were as well as Gran'dad did. I didn't like my job a bit, but I knew if I waited to go roun' by the bridge that I'd be too late to see anything that happened. So I screwed up courage an' started over. My legs ain't as long as a grown-up's and at the third step I missed the stone an' soused one leg in the water up to my knee. Gee! that was a cold one. But I wouldn't give up, an' kep' on until jus' in the middle, where the water were roarin' the worst, I slipped with both legs and went in to my waist. That settled it for me. I thought I'd drown, for a minute, but I went crazy with fear an' the next thing I knew I was standin' on the bank where I'd come from an' the cold wind was freezin' a sheet of ice on my legs an' body.

"There wasn't no time to lose. Whatever was happenin' over to the big house didn't mean as much to me as death did, an' death was on my track if I didn't get back home afore I froze stiff. I started to run. It ain't far—look there, Josie, ye could almost make it in three jumps—but I remember fallin' down half a dozen times in the snow, an' at the last I crawled to the door on my hands an' knees an' had jus' strength enough to rise up an' lift the latch.

"Gran'dad's awful stingy about burnin' wood, but I threw the chunks into the stove till the old thing roared like a furnace an' when I'd thawed out some I got off my shoes an' stockin's an' my wet dress an' put another skirt on. Then I lay in Gran'dad's chair afore the fire an' shivered an' cried like a baby whenever I thought o' that icy river.

"I guess I must 'a' went to sleep, afterwards, fer when I woke up the fire was gett'n' low an' Ol' Swallertail opened the door on a sudden an' walked in. Josie, ye orter seen him! His legs was wet an' icy, too, so he must 'a' slipped on the stones himself; an' he was shakin' all over as if he'd got the ague. His face was a dirty white an' his eyes burnt like two coals. He threw on more wood, reckless-like, an' jerked off his shoes an' socks an' set down t'other side the stove. Neither of us said noth'n' fer awhile an' then he looks at me sort o' curious an' asks:

"'Did ye git across, Ingua?'"

"'No,' says I. 'I near got drowned, tryin' it.'"

"Then he set silent ag'in, lookin' at the fire. By-'n'-by says he: 'Ingua, yer old enough to hev sense, an' I want ye to think keerful on what I'm goin' ter say. Folks aroun' here don't like you an' me very much, an' if they got a chance—or even thought they had a chance—they'd crush us under heel like they would scorpions. That's 'cause we're Craggs, for Craggs ain't never be'n poplar in this neighborhood, for some reason. Now lis'n. I've done with Ned Joselyn. It ain't nay fault as I've cast him off; it's his'n. He's got a bad heart an' he's robbed me right an' left. I could fergive him fer that, because—well, ye don't need to know why I clung to the feller when I knew he was a scoundrel. But he robbed a cause dearer to my heart than myself, an' for that I couldn't fergive him. Nobody knows Ned were here to-night, Ingua, so if anybody asks ye questions ye didn't see him at all. Fix that firm in yer mind. Ye don't know noth'n' 'bout Ned sence he went away las' October. Ye hain't seen him. Stick to that, girl, an' yer all right; but if ye blab—if ye ever tell a soul as Ned were here—I'll hev to kill yer myself, to stop yer mouth. Fix that in yer mind, too.'

"I was so skeered that I jes' looked at him. Then I says in a whisper: 'What did ye do to Ned, Gran'dad?'"

"He turned his eyes on me so fierce that I dropped my head.

Edith Van Dyne

"'I didn't kill him, if that's what ye mean,' says he. 'I orter strangled him, but I didn't want to swing fer no common thief like Ned Joselyn. Besides, he's—but that's none o' yer business. So I threatened him, an' that was jus' as good as killin'. He won't show up ag'in here, never; an' he ain't likely to show up anywheres else that he's known. P'raps he'll be hunted for, but he'll keep out a' the way. You an' I ain't got noth'n' to worry about, Ingua—unless you blab.'"

"I didn't believe a word he said, Josie. They was jus' words, an' it was nat'ral he'd lie about that night's work. When I went to bed it was near mornin', but Ol' Swallertail was still sett'n' by the fire.

"Nex' day he went on jus' as usual, an' from then till now he's never spoke to me of that night. In a couple o' weeks we heard as Ned Joselyn had run away. His wife come down here askin' fer him, but nobody'd seen hide ner hair of him. That's all, Josie; that's the whole story, an' I'm glad you know it now as well as I do. Wha' d'ye think? Did Ol' Swallertail kill Ned Joselyn?"

Josie woke from her meditation with a start.

"I—I'm going to think it over," she said evasively. "It's a queer story, Ingua—mighty queer—and it's going to take a lot of thought before I make up my mind about it."

CHAPTER XII

THEORIES ARE DANGEROUS

"What were you and Ingua talking about for so long?" asked Mary Louise, when she and Josie were alone.

"She was telling me her story," was the reply.

"All of it?"

"Every bit of it, I think."

"Oh, what was it all about?" questioned Mary Louise eagerly.

"I've promised not to tell."

"Not even me, Josie?"

"Not even you. Ingua insisted; and, really, dear, it's better you should know nothing just at present."

"Am I to be left out of all this thrilling mystery?" demanded Mary Louise with an aggrieved air.

"There won't be a thrill in it, until the end, and perhaps not

Edith Van Dyne

then. But you shall come in at the finish, if not before; I'll promise that."

"Won't this enforced promise to Ingua tie your hands?" queried the other girl, thoughtfully.

"No. I didn't promise not to act, but only to keep the child's secret. For Ingua's sake, as well as to satisfy your curiosity— and my own—I'm going to delve to the bottom of Ned Joselyn's disappearance. That will involve the attempt to discover all about Old Swallowtail, who is a mystery all by himself. I shall call on you to help me, at times, Mary Louise, but you're not to be told what is weighing so heavily on poor Ingua's mind."

"Well," said Mary Louise, "if I may help, that will serve to relieve my disappointment to an extent. But I'm surprised at Ingua. I thought she loved and trusted me."

"So she does," asserted Josie. "Since I've heard the story, I'm not surprised at Ingua at all. If you knew all, my dear, you would realize why she believes that one confidant is enough. Indeed, I'm rather surprised that Ingua ventured to confide in me."

"Is it so serious, then?"

"If her fears are justified," replied Josie gravely, "it is *very* serious."

"But *are* they justified?" urged Mary Louise.

"Ingua is a child, and very sensitive to impressions. But she is a shrewd child and, living a lonely life, has had ample time to consider the problems that confront her. Whether she is right or wrong in her conjectures, time will determine. But don't question me further, please, or you will embarrass me. To-morrow I want to go to the city, which is the county seat. Will you go with me? And can we get Uncle Eben to drive us over in the car?"

"I'll ask Gran'pa Jim."

Colonel Hathaway was rather amused at the efforts of the two girls to fathom the mystery of Old Swallowtail, but he was willing to assist in any practical way. So Uncle Eben drove them to the county seat next day and Josie spent several hours in the county clerk's office and paid a visit to the chief of police, who knew her father, John O'Gorman, by reputation. Mary Louise shopped leisurely while her friend was busy with her investigations and at last they started for home, where they arrived in time for dinner. On the way, Mary Louise inquired if Josie had secured any information of importance.

"A little," said the girl detective. "For one thing, old Hezekiah Cragg pays taxes on just one bit of land besides that little homestead of his. It is a five-acre tract, but the assessment puts it at an astonishingly low valuation—scarcely ten per cent of the value of all surrounding property. That strikes me as queer. I've got the plat of it and to-morrow we will look it up."

They found it was not easy to locate that five acres, even with a map, when the two girls made the attempt the next forenoon. But finally, at the end of a lonely lane about a mile and a half from the village, they came upon a stony tract hemmed in by low hills, which seemed to fit the location described. The place was one mass of tumbled rocks. Little herbage of any sort grew there and its low assessment value was easily explained. The surrounding farms, all highly cultivated, backed up to the little waste valley, which was fenced out—or rather in—by the owners of the fertile lands. One faintly trodden path led from the bars of the lane the girls were in toward Mr. Cragg's five acres of stones, but amid the jumble of rocks it would be difficult to walk at all.

"This is an odd freak of nature," remarked Josie, gazing at the waste with a puzzled expression. "It is easy to understand why Mr. Cragg hasn't sold this lot, as he did all his other land. No one would buy it."

"Haven't the stones a value, for building or something?" asked Mary Louise.

"Not in this location, so far from a railway. In my judgment the tract is absolutely worthless. I wonder that so economical a man as Mr. Cragg pays taxes on it."

They went no farther than the edge of the rock-strewn field, for there was nothing more to see. Up the slope of the hill, on the far side from where they stood, were jumbled masses of huge slabs and boulders that might be picturesque but were not especially interesting. The girls turned and retraced their steps to the neglected lane and from thence reached the main road again.

"I have now satisfied myself on two counts," was Josie's comment. "First, that Mr. Cragg owns no property but this stone-yard and his little home, and second, that within the last forty years he has at different times disposed of seventy thousand dollars worth of land left him by his father. The county records prove that. The last sale was made about four years ago, so he has consistently turned all his real estate into ready money."

"What can he have done with so much money?" exclaimed Mary Louise.

"Ah, that is part of the mystery, my dear. If he still has it, then the man is a miser. If he has lost it, he is a gambler, which is just about as bad. Either way, Hezekiah Cragg is not entitled to our admiration, to say the least. Let us admit that in a big city a man might lose seventy thousand dollars in business ventures without exciting adverse criticism except for a lack of judgment; but Old Swallowtail has never left Cragg's Crossing, according to all reports, and I'm sure there is no way for him to squander a fortune here."

"I think he must be a miser," said Mary Louise with conviction. "Ingua once told me of seeing lots of money pass between him and Mr. Joselyn. And—tell me, Josie—what is all his voluminous correspondence about?"

"I'm going to investigate that presently," replied her friend. "It isn't quite in line yet but will come pretty soon. To-morrow I shall call upon Old Swallowtail at his office."

"Shall you, really? And may I go with, you, Josie?"

"Not this time. You'd spoil my excuse, you see, for you are going to discharge your sewing-girl, and your sewing-girl is going to apply to Hezekiah Cragg for work. His grand-daughter needs some sewing done, by the looks of her wardrobe."

"Oh. Very well. But you will tell me what happens?"

"Of course."

"Once," said Mary Louise, "I proposed going myself to Mr. Cragg, to intercede for Ingua, but the girl thought I would do more harm than good. So I abandoned the idea."

"I think that was wise. I don't expect to get much out of the

Edith Van Dyne

man except an interview, with a chance to study him at close range. Also I'm anxious to see what that mysterious office looks like."

Mary Louise regarded her friend admiringly.

"You're very brave, Josie," she said.

"Pooh! There's no danger. One of the first things father taught me about the detective business was that all men belong to one tribe, and the criminal is inevitably a coward at heart. Old Swallowtail may be afraid of *me,* before I'm through with this case, but whether he proves guilty or innocent I shall never fear him a particle."

"Have you any theory, as yet, Josie?"

"No. Theories are dangerous things and never should be indulged in until backed by facts."

"But do not theories often lead to facts? And how about those 'O'Gorman theories' you mentioned, which you were eager to test?"

"Those are mere theories of investigation—methods to be pursued in certain situations. I believe I shall be able to test some of them in this case. My plan is to find out all I can about everyone and everything, and then marshal my facts against the question involved. If there is no answer, I've got to learn more. If I can't learn more, then the whole thing becomes mere guesswork—in other words, theory—more likely to be wrong than right."

Mary Louise seldom argued with Josie's decisions. When, the next morning, her friend started for the village to call upon Old Swallowtail, she pressed her hand and wished her good luck. Josie departed in her plain gingham dress, shoes run over at the heels, hair untidy and uncovered by hat or hood—a general aspect of slovenly servitude.

Mr. Cragg was never an early riser. He breakfasted at eight o'clock and at half past eight stalked with stiff dignity to town and entered his office without deigning to recognize any villagers he might meet. Josie was aware of this habit. She timed her visit for half-past ten.

Unnoticed she passed through the village street and crept up the stairs at the end of the store building. Before the door marked "H. Cragg, Real Estate" she paused to listen. No sound came from within, but farther along the passage she heard the dull rumble of Miss Huckins' sewing machine.

For once Josie hesitated, but realizing that hesitation meant weakness on such an errand she boldly thrust out a hand and attempted to turn the doorknob.

Edith Van Dyne

CHAPTER XIII

BLUFF AND REBUFF

The door was locked. Immediately Josie pounded upon it with her knuckles and a voice demanded:

"Who is there?"

Instead of replying, Josie knocked again, and suddenly the door was opened and Old Swallowtail stood before her.

"I—I beg your pardon," said she diffidently; "are you the real estate man?"

"Yes," he replied, standing quietly in the doorway.

"Then you're the man I want to see," she asserted and took a step forward. But he did not move an inch from his position and his eyes were fixed steadfastly on her face.

"I have nothing to sell, at present," he remarked.

"But I want to give you something to sell," she retorted impatiently, summoning her wits to meet the occasion. "Let me in, please. Or do you transact all your business in the hallway?"

Somewhat to her surprise he stepped back and held the door for her to enter. Josie promptly walked in and sat down near a round table, one comprehensive glance fixing in her mind the entire contents of the small room.

There was one window, dim and unwashed, facing the street. It had a thick shade, now raised. Originally the room had been square, and rather crudely plastered and wallpapered, but a wooden partition had afterward been erected to cut the room into two, so that the portion she had entered was long and narrow. Its sole furniture consisted of the round table, quite bare, two or three wooden-bottomed chairs, and against one wall a rack filled with books. During the interview she noted that these books were mostly directories of the inhabitants of various prominent cities in the United States, and such a collection astonished her and aroused her curiosity.

Just at present, however, the partition proved the most interesting thing she observed, for beyond it must be another room which was doubtless the particular sanctum of Old Swallowtail and to which she scarcely expected to gain admittance. The door was closed. It was stout and solid and was fitted with both an ordinary door-lock and a hasp and padlock, the latter now hanging on a nail beside the door.

This much Josie's sharp eyes saw in her first glance, but immediately her attention was demanded by Mr. Cragg, who took a seat opposite her and said in a quiet, well modulated voice: "Now, my girl, state your business." She had planned to tell him how she had come to town to sew for Mary Louise Burrows, how she had now finished her work but was so charmed with Cragg's Crossing that she did not care to leave it during the hot weather to return to the stuffy city. Therefore, she intended to add, if he would let her make some new dresses for Ingua, she would work for half her regular wages. Her dress as a sewing-girl would carry out this deception and the bait of small wages ought to interest the old man. But this clever plan had suddenly gone glimmering, for in order to gain admittance to the office and secure an interview with Old Swallowtail she had inadvertently stated that she had some real estate to dispose of. So sudden a change of base required the girl to think quickly in order to formulate a new argument that would hold his attention.

To gain time she said, slowly:

"My name is Josie Jessup. I'm a sewing-girl by profession."

"Yes, I know," he replied.

"I've been here ten days or so, working for Miss Burrows."

"I have seen you here," said Mr. Cragg.

She wondered how he knew so much, as he had never seemed to favor her with even a glance when by chance they met in the street. But perhaps Ingua had told him.

"I like Cragg's Crossing," continued Josie, assuming a confidential tone, "and I've made up my mind I'd like to live here. There ought to be plenty of work sewing for the farmers' wives, outside of what Miss Huckins does, and it don't cost much to live in a small town. In the city I own a little house and lot left to me by my uncle on my mother's side, and I've decided to trade it for some place here. Don't you know, sir, of someone who'd like to move to the city, and will be glad to make the exchange?"

"I know of no such person," he replied coldly.

"But you will make inquiries?"

"It would be useless. I am very busy to-day, so if you will excuse me—"

He rose and bowed.

Josie was disappointed. She decided to revert to her first proposition.

"Doesn't your granddaughter need some sewing done, sir?" she asked, with a frank look from her innocent blue eyes.

He stood still, silently studying her face. With one hand he rubbed his chin gently, as if in thought. Then he said:

"We cannot afford to hire our sewing done, but I thank you for the offer. Good morning, Miss—Jessup."

Walking to the door he held it open and bowed gravely as she walked out. Next moment she heard the key click as it turned in the lock.

Josie, feeling a sense of failure, slowly went down the stairs, entered the store and perched herself upon the sugar-barrel. Old Sol was waiting on a farmer's wife and only gave the girl a glance.

Josie reflected on her interview with Mr. Cragg while it was fresh in her mind. He was no crude, uneducated country bumpkin, despite his odd ways and peculiar dress. Indeed, the man had astonished her by his courtesy, his correct method of speech, his perfect self-assurance. Her visit was calculated to annoy him and to arouse his impatience. After Ingua's report of him she expected he would become scornful or sarcastic or even exhibit violent anger; yet there had been nothing objectionable in his manner or words. Still, he had dismissed her as abruptly as possible and was not eager to grasp an opportunity to exchange real estate.

"That isn't his business at all," she told herself. "It's merely a blind, although he actually did rent the Kenton Place to Colonel Hathaway...I wonder what he does in that office all day. In the inner room, of course. That is his real workshop...He's quite gentlemanly. He has a certain amount of breeding, which Ingua wholly lacks....He must realize what a crude and uncultured little thing his granddaughter is. Then why hasn't he tried to train her differently?...Really, he quite awed me with his stately, composed manner. No one would expect that sort of man to be a murderer. But—there! haven't I been warned that the educated gentleman is the worst type of criminal, and the most difficult to detect?"

Sol's customer went away and the old man approached the barrel.

"Well," he said, "wanter buy anything to-day?"

"No," said Josie pleasantly, "this is only a social call. I've just come from Old Swallow-tail's office and thought a word with you would cheer me up."

"You! You be'n to Ol' Swallertail's office! Sakes alive, gal, I wouldn't dare do that myself."

"Why not?"

"He goes crazy when he gits mad."

"Are you sure of that?"

"Ev'rybody here knows it, from the three-year-olds up. What

did ye go to him for?"

"A little matter of business."

"An' he slammed the door in yer face?"

"No, indeed."

"That's funny," said old Sol, rubbing his forehead in a perplexed way.

"He was very decent to me," continued Josie. "Acted like a gentleman. Talked as if he'd been to school, you know."

"School? Well, I should say he had!" exclaimed the store-keeper. "Ol' Swallertail's the most eddicated man in these 'ere parts, I guess. Ol' Nick Cragg, his daddy, wanted for him to be a preacher—or a priest, most likely—an' when he was a boy his ol' man paid good money to hev him eddicated at a the—at a theo—at a collidge. But Hezekiah wa'n't over-religious, an' 'lowed he didn't hev no call to preach; so that's all the good the eddication ever done him."

"*You've* never felt the need of an education, have you?" asked the girl, artlessly.

"Me? Well, I ain't sayin' as I got no eddication, though I don't class myself in book-l'arnin' with Ol' Swallertail. Three winters I went to school, an' once I helped whip the school-teacher. Tain't ev'ry one has got *that* record. But eddication means more'n books; it means keepin' yer eyes open an' gitt'n' onter the tricks o' yer trade. Ev'ry time I git swindled, I've l'arned somethin', an' if I'd started this store in New York instid o' Cragg's Crossin', they might be runnin' me fer president by this time."

"But what could Cragg's Crossing have done without you?" inquired Josie. "It seems to me you're needed here."

"Well, that's worth thinkin' on," admitted the storekeeper. "And as for Old Swallowtail, he may have learned some tricks of his trade too. But I don't know what his trade is."

"Nobody knows that. I don't b'lieve that business o' his'n is a trade at all; I'll bet it's a steal, whatever its other name happens to be."

"But he doesn't prosper."

"No; he ain't got much t' show fer all these years. Folks used to think he'd got money saved from the sale of his land, till Ned Joselyn come here an' dallied with Ol' Swallertail's savin's an' then took to the woods. It's gener'ly b'lieved that what Cragg had once Ned's got now; but it don't matter much. Cragg hain't got long ter live an' his feed don't cost him an' his little gal much more'n it costs to feed my cat."

There was no further information to be gleaned from Sol Jerrems, so Josie walked home.

CHAPTER XIV

MIDNIGHT VIGILS

"Well, how is our girl detective progressing in her discovery of crime and criminals?" asked Colonel Hathaway that evening, as they sat in the living-room after dinner.

"Don't call me a girl detective, please," pleaded Josie O'Gorman. "I'm only an apprentice at the trade, Colonel, and I have never realized more than I do at this moment the fact that I've considerable to learn before I may claim member-ship with the profession."

"Then you're finding your present trail a difficult one to follow?"

"I believe my stupidity is making it difficult," admitted Josie, with a sigh. "Father would scold me soundly if he knew how foolishly I behaved to-day. There was every opportunity of my forcing a clew by calling unexpectedly on Mr. Cragg at his office, but he defeated my purpose so easily that now I'm wondering if he suspects who I am, and why I'm here. He couldn't have been more cautious."

"He could scarcely suspect that," said the Colonel, musingly. "But I've noticed that these simple country people are chary of confiding in strangers."

"Ah, if Mr. Cragg were only that—a simple, unlettered countryman, as I thought him—I should know how to win his confidence. But, do you know, sir, he is well educated and intelligent. Once he studied for the priesthood or ministry, attending a theological college."

"Indeed!"

"My informant, the village authority—who is Sol Jerrems the storekeeper—says he objected to becoming a priest at the last because he had no leaning that way. My own opinion is that he feared his ungovernable temper would lead to his undoing. I am positive that his hysterical fury, when aroused, has gotten him into trouble many times, even in this patient community."

"That's it," said Mary Louise with conviction; "his temper has often made him cruel to poor Ingua, and perhaps his temper caused unfortunate Ned Joselyn to disappear."

"Have you discovered anything more than you have told me?" she asked.

"Not a thing," replied Mary Louise. "I'm waiting for *you* to make discoveries, Josie."

"A puzzle that is readily solved," remarked the Colonel, picking up his book, "is of little interest. The obstacles you are meeting, Josie, incline me to believe you girls have unearthed a real mystery. It is not a mystery of the moment, however, so take your time to fathom it. The summer is young yet."

Josie went to her room early, saying she was tired, but as

soon as she was alone and free she slipped on a jacket and stealthily left the house. Down the driveway she crept like a shadow, out through the gates, over the bridge, and then she turned down the pathway leading to Old Swallowtail's cottage.

"The stepping-stones are a nearer route," she reflected, "but I don't care to tackle them in the dark."

The cottage contained but three rooms. The larger one downstairs was a combination kitchen and dining room. A small wing, built upon one side, was used by Mr. Cragg for his private apartment, but its only outlet was through the main room. At the back was a lean-to shed, in which was built a narrow flight of stairs leading to a little room in the attic, where Ingua slept. Josie knew the plan of the house perfectly, having often visited Ingua during the day when her grandfather was absent and helped her sweep and make the beds and wash the dishes.

To-night Josie moved noiselessly around the building, satisfied herself that Ingua was asleep and that Mr. Cragg was still awake, and then strove to peer through the shuttered window to discover what the old man was doing.

She found this impossible. Although the weather was warm the window was tightly shut and a thick curtain was drawn across it.

Josie slipped over to the river bank and in the shadow of a tree sat herself down to watch and wait with such patience as she could muster. It was half past nine o'clock, and Ingua had told her that when her grandfather was wakeful, and indulged in his long walks, he usually left the house between ten o'clock and midnight—seldom earlier and never later. He would go to bed, the child said, and finding he could not sleep, would again dress and go out into the night, only to return at early morning.

Josie doubted that he ever undressed on such occasions, knowing, as he no doubt did, perfectly well what his program for the night would be. She had decided that the nocturnal excursions were not due to insomnia but were carefully planned to avoid possible observation. When all the countryside was wrapped in slumber the old gentleman stole from his cottage and went—where? Doubtless to some secret place that had an important bearing on his life and occupation. It would be worth while, Josie believed, to discover the object of these midnight excursions. Ingua claimed that her grandfather's periods of wakeful walking were irregular; sometimes he would be gone night after night, and then for weeks he would remain at home and sleep like other folks.

So Josie was not surprised when old Swallowtail's light was extinguished shortly after ten o'clock and from then until midnight he had not left the house. Evidently this was not one of his "wakeful" periods. The girl's eyes, during this time, never left the door of the cottage. The path to the bridge passed her scarcely five yards distant. Therefore, as Hezekiah Cragg had not appeared, he was doubtless sleeping the sleep of the just—or the unjust, for all sorts and conditions of men indulge in sleep.

Josie waited until nearly one o'clock. Then she went home, let herself in by a side door to which she had taken the key, and in a few minutes was as sound asleep as Old Swallowtail ought to be.

For three nights in succession the girl maintained this vigil, with no result whatever. It was wearisome work and she began to tire of it. On the fourth day, as she was "visiting" with Ingua, she asked:

"Has your grandfather had any sleepless nights lately?"

"I don't know," was the reply. "But he ain't walked any, as he sometimes does, for I hain't heard him go out."

"Do you always hear him?"

"P'r'aps not always, but most times."

"And does he walk more than one night?" inquired Josie.

"When he takes them fits, they lasts for a week or more," asserted Ingua. "Then, for a long time, he sleeps quiet."

"Will you let me know, the next time he takes to walking?"

"Why?" asked the child, suspiciously.

"It's a curious habit," Josie explained, "and I'd like to know what he does during all those hours of the night."

"He walks," declared Ingua; "and, if he does anything else, it's his own business."

"I've wondered," said Josie impressively, "if he doesn't visit some hidden grave during those midnight rambles."

Ingua shuddered.

"I wish ye wouldn't talk like that," she whispered. "It gives me the creeps."

"Wouldn't you like to know the truth of all this mystery, Ingua?"

Edith Van Dyne

"Sometimes I would, an' sometimes I wouldn't. If the truth leaked out, mebbe Gran'dad would git inter a lot o' trouble. I don't want that, Josie. I ain't no cause to love Gran'dad, but he's a Cragg an' I'm a Cragg, an' no Cragg ever went back on the fambly."

It seemed unwise to urge the child further to betray her grandfather, yet for Ingua's sake, if for no other reason, Josie was determined to uncover the hidden life of Hezekiah Cragg.

The following night she watched again at her station by the river bank, and again the midnight hour struck and the old man had not left his cottage. His light was extinguished at eleven o'clock. At twelve-thirty Josie rose from the shadow of the tree and slowly walked to the bridge. There, instead of going home, she turned in the direction of the town.

In the sky were a few stars and the slim crescent of a new moon, affording sufficient light to guide her steps. Crickets chirped and frogs in the marshes sang their hoarse love songs, but otherwise an intense stillness pervaded the countryside. You must not consider Josie O'Gorman an especially brave girl, for she had no thought of fear in such solitary wanderings. Although but seventeen years of age, she had been reared from early childhood in an atmosphere of intrigue and mystery, for her detective father had been accustomed to argue his cases and their perplexities with his only child and for hours at a time he would instruct her in all the details of his profession. It was O'Gorman's ambition that his daughter might become a highly proficient female detective.

"There are so many cases where a woman is better than a man," he would say, "and there is such a lack of competent women in this important and fascinating profession, that I am promoting the interests of both my daughter and the public safety by training Josie to become a good detective."

And the girl, having been her father's confidant since she was able to walk and talk, became saturated with detective lore and only needed practical experience and more mature judgment fully to justify O'Gorman's ambition for her.

However, the shrewd old secret service officer well knew that the girl was not yet ready to be launched into active service. The experience she needed was only to be gained in just such odd private cases as the one on which she was now engaged, so he was glad to let her come to Cragg's Crossing, and Josie was glad to be there. She was only content when "working," and however the Cragg mystery developed or resulted, her efforts to solve it were sure to sharpen her wits and add to her practical knowledge of her future craft.

When she reached the town she found it absolutely deserted. Not a light shone anywhere; no watchman was employed; the denizens of Cragg's Crossing were all in bed and reveling in dreamland.

Josie sat on the bottom stair of the flight leading to the store and removed her shoes. Upstairs the family of Sol Jerrems and Miss Huckins the dressmaker were sleeping and must not be disturbed. The girl made no sound as she mounted the stairs and softly stole to the door of H. Cragg's real estate office. Here it was dark as could be, but Josie drew some skeleton keys from her pocket and slid them, one by one, into the lock. The fourth key fitted; she opened the door silently and having entered the room drew the door shut behind her.

The thick shade was drawn over the window. It was as black here as it was in the hallway. Josie flashed a small searchlight on the door of the connecting room and saw that it was not only locked in the ordinary manner but that the padlock she had noted on her former visit to the room was now inserted in the hasp and formed an additional security against intrusion.

While her electric spotlight played upon this padlock she bent over and examined it swiftly but with care.

"A Yale lock," she muttered. "It can't be picked, but it will delay me for only a few minutes."

Then from her pocket she brought out a small steel hacksaw, and as she could not work the saw and hold the flashlight at the same time she went to the window and removed the heavy shade. The light that now came into the room was dim, but sufficient for her purpose. Returning to the door of the mysterious inner room, the contents of which she had determined to investigate, she seized the padlock firmly with one hand while with the other she began to saw through the steel loop that passed through the hasp.

The sound made by the saw was so slight that it did not worry her, but another sound, of an entirely different character and coming from the hallway, caused her to pause and glance over her shoulder.

Slowly the outer door opened and a form appeared in the doorway. It was a mere shadow, at first, but it deliberately advanced to the table, struck a match and lighted a small kerosene lamp.

She was face to face with Old Swallowtail.

CHAPTER XV

"OLD SWALLOWTAIL"

Josie was so astonished that she still bent over the lock, motionless, saw in hand. In the instant she made a mental review of her proceedings and satisfied herself that she had been guilty of no professional blunder. The inopportune appearance of Mr. Cragg must be attributed to a blind chance—to fate. So the first wave of humiliation that swept over her receded as she gathered her wits to combat this unexpected situation.

Mr. Cragg stood by the table looking at her. He was very calm. The discovery of the girl had not aroused that violence of temper for which the old man was noted. Josie straightened up, slipped the saw in her pocket and faced him unflinchingly.

"Won't you sit down?" he said, pointing to a chair beside her. "I would like to know why you have undertaken to rob me."

Josie sat down, her heart bounding with joy. If he mistook her for a thief all was not lost and she would not have to write "finis" as yet to this important case. But she made no answer to his remark; she merely stared at him in a dull, emotionless way that was cleverly assumed.

Edith Van Dyne

"I suppose," he continued, "you have been told I am rich—a miser—and perhaps you imagine I keep my wealth in that little room, because I have taken pains to secure it from intrusion by prying meddlers. I suspected you, my girl, when you came to see me the other day. Your errand was palpably invented. You wanted to get the lay of the room, in preparation for this night's work. But who told you I was worthy of being robbed? Was it Ingua?"

"No," came a surly reply. "She won't mention you to me."

"Very good. But the neighbors—the busy-bodies around here? Perhaps old Sol Jerrems has gossiped of my supposed hoard. Is it not so?"

Josie dropped her eyes as if confused but remained silent. The old man seemed to regard her as a curiosity, for his cold gray eyes examined her person with the same expression with which he might have regarded a caged monkey.

"Then you do not wish to confess?"

"What's the use?" she demanded with a burst of impatience. "Haven't you caught me at the job?"

He continued to eye her, reflectively.

"The cities breed felons," he remarked. "It is a pity so young a girl should have chosen so dangerous and disastrous a career. It is inevitably disastrous. How did it happen that Colonel Hathaway allowed you to impose on him?"

"I do sewing," she said doggedly.

"In order to gain entrance to a household, I suppose. But Hathaway is wealthy. Why did you not undertake to rob him, instead of me?"

"One at a time," said Josie, with a short laugh.

"Oh, I understand. You expected to make the small pick-ups and then land the grand coup. The answer is simple, after all. But," he added, his voice growing stern and menacing for the first time, "I do not intend to be robbed, my girl. Fleece Hathaway if you can; it is none of my business; but you must not pry into my personal affairs or rifle my poor rooms. Do you understand me?"

"I—I think so, sir."

"Avoid me, hereafter. Keep out of my path. The least interference from you, in any way, will oblige me to turn you over to the police."

"You'll let me go, now?"

He glanced at her, frowning.

"I am too much occupied to prosecute you—unless you annoy me further. Perhaps you have this night learned a lesson that will induce you to abandon such desperate, criminal ventures."

Josie stood up.

"I wish I knew how you managed to catch me," she said, with a sigh.

"You were watching my house to-night, waiting until I was safely in bed before coming here. I happened to leave my room for a little air, and going out my back door I passed around the house and stood at the corner, in deep shade. My

Edith Van Dyne

eyes were good enough to distinguish a form lurking under the tree by the river bank. I went in, put out my light, and returned to my former position. You watched the house and I watched you. You are not very clever, for all your slyness. You will never be clever enough to become a good thief— meaning a successful thief. After a half hour I saw you rise and take the path to the village. I followed you. Do you understand now? God has protected the just and humbled the wicked."

That final sentence surprised the girl. Coming from his lips, it shocked her. In his former speech he had not denounced her crime, but only her indiscretion and the folly of her attempt. Suddenly he referred to God as his protector, asserting his personal uprightness as warrant for Divine protection; and, singularly enough, his tone was sincere.

Josie hesitated whether to go or not, for Old Swallowtail seemed in a talkative mood and she had already discovered a new angle to his character. By way of diversion she began to cry.

"I—I know I'm wicked," she sobbed; "it's wrong to steal; I know it is. But I—I—need the money, and you've got lots of it; and—and—I thought you must be just as wicked as I am!"

His expression changed to one of grim irony.

"Yes," said he, "by common report I am guilty of every sin in the calendar. Do you know why?"

"No; of course I don't!" she answered, softening her sobs to hear more clearly.

"Years ago, when I was a young man, I stabbed a fellow-student in the neck—a dreadful wound—because he taunted me about my mode of dress. I was wearing the only clothes my eccentric father would provide me with. I am wearing the same style of costume yet, as penance for that dastardly act—caused by an ungovernable temper with which I have been cursed from my birth. I would have entered the service of God had it not been for that temper. I am unable to control it, except by avoiding undue contact with my fellow men. That is why. I am living here, a recluse, when I should be taking an active part in the world's work."

He spoke musingly, as if to himself more than to the girl who hung on each word with eager interest. No one had ever told her as much of Old Swallowtail as he was now telling her of himself. She wondered why he was so confidential. Was it because she seemed dull and stupid? Because she was a stranger who was likely to decamp instantly when he let her go? Or was the retrospective mood due to the hour and the unwonted situation? She waited, scarce breathing lest she lose a word.

"The poor fellow whom I stabbed lived miserably for twenty years afterward," he went on, "and I supported him and his family during that time, for his life had been ruined by my act. Later in life and here at the Crossing, people saw me kill a balky horse in a wild rage, and they have been afraid of me ever since. Even more recently I—"

He suddenly paused, remembering where he was and to whom he was speaking. The girl's face was perfectly blank when he shot a shrewd glance at it. Her look seemed to relieve his embarrassment.

"However," said he in a different tone, "I am not so black as I'm painted."

"I don't think you treat poor Ingua quite right," remarked Josie.

"Eh? Why not?"

"You neglect her; you don't give her enough to eat; she hasn't a dress fit for a ragamuffin to wear. And she's your granddaughter."

He drew in a long breath, staring hard.

"Has she been complaining?"

"Not to me," said Josie; "but she doesn't need to. Haven't I eyes? Doesn't everyone say it's a shame to treat the poor child the way you do? My personal opinion is that you're a poor excuse for a grandfather," she added, with more spirit than she had yet exhibited.

He sat silent a long time, looking at the lamp. His face was hard; his long, slim fingers twitched as if longing to throttle someone; but he positively ignored Josie's presence. She believed he was struggling to subdue what Ingua called "the devils," and would not have been surprised had he broken all bounds and tried to do her an injury.

"Go!" he said at last, still without looking at her. "Go, and remember that I will not forgive twice."

She thought it best to obey. Very softly she left the room, and as she passed out he was still staring at the flame of the lamp and alternately clenching and unclenching his talon-like fingers.

CHAPTER XVI

INGUA'S NEW DRESS

"Well," said Mary Louise, when Josie had related to her friend the story next morning, "what do you think of Old Swallowtail now?"

"About the same as before. I'm gradually accumulating facts to account for the old man's strange actions, but I'm not ready to submit them for criticism just yet. The plot is still a bit ragged and I want to mend the holes before I spread it out before you."

"Do you think he suspects who you are?"

"No; he thinks I'm a waif from the city with a penchant for burglary. He expects me to rob you, presently, and then run away. I'm so unlikely to cross his path again that he talked with unusual frankness to me—or *at* me, if you prefer to put it that way. All I gained last night was the knowledge that he's afraid of himself, that his temper cost him a career in the world and obliged him to live in seclusion and that he has a secret which he doesn't intend any red-headed girl to stumble on accidentally."

"And you think he was angry when you accused him of

neglecting Ingua?"

"I'm sure he was. It made him more furious than my attempt to saw his padlock. Come, let's run over and see Ingua now. I want to ask how her grandfather treated her this morning."

They walked through the grounds, crossed the river on the stepping-stones and found Ingua just finishing her morning's work. The child greeted them eagerly.

"I'm glad you come," she said, "for I was meanin' to run over to your place pretty soon. What d'ye think hes happened? Las' night, in the middle o' the night—or p'r'aps nearer mornin'—Gran'dad begun to slam things aroun'. The smashin' of tables an' chairs woke me up, but I didn't dare go down to see what was the matter. He tumbled ev'rything 'round in the kitchen an' then went inter his own room an' made the fur fly there. I knew he were in one o' his tantrums an' that he'd be sorry if he broke things, but it wasn't no time to interfere. When the rumpus stopped I went to sleep ag'in, but I got up early an' had his breakfas' all ready when he come from his room. I'd picked up all the stuff he'd scattered an' mended a broken chair, an' things didn't look so bad.

"Well, Ol' Swallertail jes' looked aroun' the room an' then at me an' sot down to eat. 'Ingua,' he says pretty soon,' you need a new dress.' Say, girls, I near fell over backwards! 'Go down to Sol Jerrems,' says he, 'an' pick out the goods, an' I'll pay for it. I'll stop in this mornin' an' tell Sol to let ye have it. An',' says he, lookin' at me ruther queer, 'ye might ask that redheaded sewin'-girl that's stay in' at the Hathaways' to make it up fer ye. I don't think she'll ask ye a cent fer the work.'

"'Gran'dad,' says I, 'would ye hev a Cragg accep' charity, even to the makin' of a dress?'"

"'No,' says he; 'the girl owes me somethin' an' I guess she'll be glad to square the account.'"

"Then he goes away to town an' I've be'n nervous an' flustered ever since. I can't make it out, I can't. Do you owe him anything, Josie?"

"Yes," said Josie with a laugh, "I believe I do. You shall have the dress, Ingua—all made up—and I'll go down with you and help pick out the goods."

"So will I!" exclaimed Mary Louise, highly delighted.

"And we will have Miss Huckins cut and fit it," continued Josie. "I'm not much good at that thing, Ingua, so we will have a real dressmaker and I'll pay her and charge it up to what I owe your grandfather."

The little girl seemed puzzled.

"How'd ye happen to owe him anything, Josie?" she asked.

"Didn't he tell you?"

"Not a word."

"Then he expects it to remain a secret, and you mustn't urge me to tell. I'm pretty good at keeping secrets, Ingua. Aren't you glad of that?"

They trooped away to town, presently, all in high spirits, and purchased the dress and trimmings at the store. Old Sol was so astonished at this transaction that he assailed the three girls with a thousand questions, to none of which did he receive a satisfactory reply.

Edith Van Dyne

"He didn't put no limit on the deal," said the storekeeper. "He jus' said: 'Whatever the gal picks out, charge it to me an' I'll pay the bill.' Looks like Ol' Swallertail hed gone plumb crazy, don't it?"

Then they went upstairs to Miss Huckins, who was likewise thrilled with excitement at the startling event of Ingua's having a new dress. Mary Louise and Josie helped plan the dress, which was to be a simple and practical affair, after all, and the dressmaker measured the child carefully and promised her a fitting the very next day.

"I don't quite understan'," remarked Ingua, as they walked home after this impressive ceremony, "why you don't make the dress yourself, Josie, an' save yer money. You're a dressmaker, ye say."

"I'm a sewing-girl," replied Josie calmly, "but I've promised Mary Louise to sew for no one but her while I'm here, and I'm too lazy to sew much, anyway. I'm having a sort of vacation, you know."

"Josie is my friend," explained Mary Louise, "and I won't let her sew at all, if I can help it. I want her to be just my companion and have a nice visit before she goes back to the city."

But when the two girls were alone Josie said to Mary Louise:

"Old Cragg isn't so stony-hearted, after all. Just my suggestion last night that Ingua was being neglected has resulted in the new dress."

"He threw things, though, before he made up his mind to be generous," observed Mary Louise. "But this proves that the old man isn't so very poor. He must have a little money, Josie."

Josie nodded her head absently. She was trying hard to understand Mr. Cragg's character, and so far it baffled her. He had frankly admitted his ungovernable temper and had deplored it. Also he had refrained from having Josie arrested for burglary because he was "too occupied to prosecute her." Occupied? Occupied with what? Surely not the real estate business. She believed the true reason for her escape was that he dreaded prominence. Old Swallowtail did not wish to become mixed up with police courts any more than he could help. This very occurrence made her doubt him more than ever.

Edith Van Dyne

CHAPTER XVII

A CLEW AT LAST

That night Josie resumed her watch of Cragg's cottage. She did not trust to the shadow of the tree to conceal her but hid herself under the bank of the river, among the dry stones, allowing only her head to project above the embankment and selecting a place where she could peer through some low bushes.

She suspected that the excitement of the previous night might render the old man nervous and wakeful and send him out on one of his midnight prowls. This suspicion seemed justified when, at eleven-thirty, his light went out and a few minutes later he turned the corner of the house and appeared in the path.

He did not seem nervous, however. With hands clasped behind his back and head bowed, he leisurely paced the path to the bridge, without hesitation crossed the river and proceeded along the road in a direction opposite to the village.

Josie was following, keeping herself concealed with utmost care. She remembered that his eyes were sharp in penetrating shadows.

He kept along the main country road for a time and then turned to the right and followed an intersecting road. Half a mile in this direction brought him to a lane running between two farm tracts but which was so little used that grass and weeds had nearly obliterated all traces of wagon-wheels.

By this time Josie's eyes were so accustomed to the dim moonlight that she could see distinctly some distance ahead of her. The sky was clear; there was just enough wind to rustle the leaves of the trees. Now and then in some farmyard a cock would crow or a dog bark, but no other sounds broke the stillness of the night.

The girl knew now where Old Swallowtail was bound. At the end of this lane lay his five acres of stones, and he was about to visit it. The fact gave her a queer little thrill of the heart, for a dozen strange fancies crossed her mind in rapid succession. If he had really killed Ned Joselyn, it was probable he had buried the man in this neglected place, amongst the rubble of stones. Josie had inspected every foot of ground on the Kenton Place and satisfied herself no grave had been dug there. Indeed, at the time of Joselyn's "disappearance" the ground had been frozen so hard that the old man could not have dug a grave. Perhaps after a night or two he had dragged the corpse here and covered it with stones. It would be a safe hiding-place.

And now regret for his act drove the murderer here night after night to watch over the secret grave.

Or, granting that the supposed crime had not been committed, might not Mr. Cragg have discovered some sort of mineral wealth in his stone-yard, which would account for his paying taxes on the place and visiting it so often? Or did he simply love the solitude of the dreary waste where, safe from prying eyes, he could sit among the rocky boulders and commune with himself beneath the moonlit sky?

Such conjectures as these occupied the girl's mind while she stealthily "shadowed" the old man along the lane. Never once did he look behind him, although she was prepared to dissolve from view instantly, had he done so. And at last the end of the lane was reached and he climbed the rail fence which separated it from the valley of stones.

Josie saw him suddenly pause, motionless, as he clung to the rails. She guessed from his attitude that he was staring straight ahead of him at something that had surprised him. A full minute he remained thus before he let himself down on the other side and disappeared from view.

The girl ran lightly forward and, crouching low, peered through the bars of the fence. Half a dozen paces distant the old man stood among the stones in a silent paroxysm of rage. He waved his long arms in the air, anon clenching his fists and shaking them at some object beyond him. His frail old body fluttered back and forth, right and left, as if he were doing a weird dance among the rocks. The violence of his emotion was something terrible to witness and fairly startled the girl. Had he screamed, or sobbed, or shrieked, or moaned, the scene would have been more bearable, but such excess of silent, intense rage, made her afraid for the first time in her life.

She wanted to run away. At one time she actually turned to fly; but then common sense came to her rescue and she resolved to stay and discover what had affected Old Swallowtail so strongly. From her present position she could see nothing more than a vista of tumbled stones, but rising until her head projected above the topmost rail she presently saw, far across the valley, an automobile, standing silhouetted against the gray background.

The machine was at present vacant. It had been driven in from the other side of the valley, where doubtless there were other lanes corresponding with the one she was in. However, there was no fence on that side to separate the lane from the waste tract, so the machine had been driven as close as possible to the edge of the stones.

Although the automobile was deserted, that was evidently the object which had aroused old Cragg's fury, the object at which he was even yet shaking his clenched fists. Josie wondered and watched. Gradually the paroxysm of wrath diminished. Presently the old man stood as motionless as the stones about him. Five minutes, perhaps, he remained thus, controlling himself by a mighty effort, regaining his capacity to think and reason. Then, to the girl's amazement, he tottered toward a large, shelf-like slab of stone and kneeling down, as before an altar, he bared his head, raised his arms on high and began to pray.

There was no mistaking this attitude. Old Swallowtail was calling on God to support him in this hour of trial. Josie felt something clutching at her heart. Nothing could be more impressive than this scene—this silent but earnest appeal to the Most High by the man whom she suspected of murder— of crimes even more terrible. She could see his eyes, pleading and sincere, turned upward; could see his gray hair flutter in the breeze; could see his lips move, though they uttered no sound. And after he had poured out his heart to his Maker he extended his arms upon the slab, rested his head upon them and again became motionless.

The girl waited. She was sorely troubled, surprised, even humiliated at being the witness of this extraordinary and varied display of emotion. She felt a sense of intrusion that was almost unjustifiable, even in a detective. What right had anyone to spy upon a communion between God and man?

He rose, at length, rose and walked uncertainly forward, stumbling among the ragged rocks. He made for the far hillside that was cluttered with huge fragments of stone, some weighing many tons and all tumbled helter-skelter as if aimlessly tossed there by some giant hand. And when he reached the place he threaded his way between several great boulders and suddenly disappeared.

Josie hesitated a moment what to do, yet instinct urged her to follow. She had a feeling that she was on the verge of an important discovery, that events were about to happen which had been wholly unforeseen even by old Cragg himself.

She was taking a serious risk by venturing on the stony ground, for under the moonlight her dark form would show distinctly against the dull gray of the stones. Yet she climbed the fence and with her eye fixed on the cluster of rocks where Old Swallowtail had disappeared she made her way as best she could toward the place. Should the old man reappear or the owner of the strange automobile emerge from the rocks Josie was sure to be discovered, and there was no telling what penalty she might be obliged to pay for spying. It was a dreary, deserted place; more than one grave might be made there without much chance of detection.

In a few minutes she had reached the hillside and was among the great boulders. She passed between the same ones where Mr. Cragg had disappeared but found so many set here and there that to follow his trail was impossible unless chance led her aright.

There were no paths, for a rubble of small stones covered the ground everywhere. Between some of the huge rocks the passage was so narrow she could scarcely squeeze through; between others there was ample space for two people to walk abreast. The girl paused frequently to listen, taking care the while to make no sound herself, but an intense silence pervaded the place.

After wandering here and there for a time without result she had started to return to the entrance of this labyrinth when her ears for the first time caught a sound—a peculiar grinding, thumping sound that came from beneath her feet seemingly, and was of so unusual a character that she was puzzled to explain its cause.

The shadows cast by the towering rocks rendered this place quite dark, so Josie crouched in the deepest shade she could find and listened carefully to the strange sound, trying to determine its origin. It was surely under ground—a little to the right of her—perhaps beneath the hillside, which slanted abruptly from this spot. She decided there must be some secret passage that led to a cave under the hill. Such a cave might be either natural or artificial; in either case she was sure old Cragg used it as a rendezvous or workshop and visited it stealthily on his "wakeful" nights.

Having located the place to the best of her ability Josie began to consider what caused that regular, thumping noise, which still continued without intermission.

"I think it must be some sort of an engine," she reflected; "a stamp for ore, or something of that sort. Still, it isn't likely there is any steam or electrical power to operate the motor of so big a machine. It might be a die stamp, though, operated by foot power, or—this is most likely—a foot-power printing-press. Well, if a die stamp or a printing press, I believe the mystery of Old Swallowtail's 'business' is readily explained."

She sat still there, crouching between the rocks, for more than two hours before the sound of the machine finally

Edith Van Dyne

ceased. Another hour passed in absolute silence. She ventured to flash her pocket searchlight upon the dial of her watch and found it was nearly four o'clock. Dawn would come, presently, and then her situation would be more precarious than ever.

While she thus reflected the sound of footsteps reached her ears—very near to her, indeed—and a voice muttered:

"Come this way. Have you forgotten?"

"Forgotten? I found the place, didn't I?" was the surly reply.

Then there passed her, so closely that she could have touched them, three dim forms. She watched them go and promptly followed, taking the chance of discovery if they looked behind. They were wholly unconscious of her presence, however, and soon made their way out into the open. There they paused, and Josie, hiding behind a high rock, could both see and hear them plainly.

One was old Cragg; another a tall, thin man with a monocle in his left eye; the third, she found to her surprise, was none other than Jim Bennett the postman. The tall man held in his arms a heavy bundle, securely wrapped.

"You'll surely get them off to-morrow?" said Cragg to him,

"Of course," was the answer. "You may be certain I'll not have them on my hands longer than is necessary."

"Do you mean to play square, this time?"

"Don't be a fool," said the tall man impatiently. "Your infernal suspicions have caused trouble enough, during the past year. Hidden like a crab in your shell, you think everything on the outside is going wrong. Can't you realize, Cragg, that I *must* be loyal to C. I. L.? There's no question of my playing square; I've got to."

"That's right, sir," broke in Jim Bennett. "Seems to me he's explained everything in a satisfactory manner—as far as anyone *could* explain."

"Then good night," said Cragg, gruffly, "and—good luck."

"Good night," growled the tall man in return and made off in the direction of the automobile, carrying the package with him. The other two stood silently watching him until he reached the car, took his seat and started the motor. Presently the machine passed out of sight and then Bennett said in a tone of deepest respect:

"Good night, Chief. This meeting was a great thing for C. I. L. It brings us all nearer to final success."

"I wish I could trust him," replied Cragg, doubtfully. "Good night, Jim."

The postman made off in another direction and the old man waited until he had fully disappeared before he walked away over the stones himself. Josie let him go. She did not care to follow him home. Weary though she was from her long vigil she determined to examine the rocks by daylight before she left the place.

The sun was just showing its rim over the hills when she quitted Hezekiah Cragg's five acres of stones and took the lane to the highway. But her step was elastic, her eyes bright, her face smiling.

"I've found the entrance, though I couldn't break in," she

Edith Van Dyne

proudly murmured. "But a little dynamite—or perhaps a few blows of an axe—will soon remove the barrier. This affair, however, is now too big and too serious for me to handle alone. I must have help. I think it will amaze dear old Dad to know what I've stumbled on this night!"

CHAPTER XVIII

DOUBTS AND SUSPICIONS

Mary Louise entered her friend's room at seven o'clock and exclaimed: "Not up yet?"

Josie raised her head drowsily from the pillow.

"Let me sleep till noon," she pleaded. "I've been out all night."

"And did you learn anything?" was the eager question.

"Please let me sleep!"

"Shall I send you up some breakfast, Josie?"

"Breakfast? Bah!"

She rolled over, drawing the clothes about her, and Mary Louise softly left the darkened room and went down to breakfast.

"Gran'pa Jim," said she, thoughtfully buttering her toast, "do you think it's right for Josie to be wandering around in the dead of night?"

He gave her an odd look and smiled.

"If I remember aright, it was one Miss Mary Louise Burrows who thrust Josie into this vortex of mystery."

"You didn't answer my question, Gran'pa Jim."

"I can imagine no harm, to girl or man, in being abroad in this peaceful country at night, if one has the nerve to undertake it. You and I, dear, prefer our beds. Josie is wrapped up in the science of criminal investigation and has the enthusiasm of youth to egg her on. Moreover, she is sensible enough to know what is best for her. I do not think we need worry over her nightly wanderings, which doubtless have an object. Has she made any important discovery as yet?"

"I believe not," said Mary Louise. "She has learned enough to be positive that old Mr. Cragg is engaged in some secret occupation of an illegal character, but so far she is unable to determine what it is. He's a very queer old man, it seems, but shrewd and clever enough to keep his secret to himself."

"And how about the disappearance of Mr. Joselyn?"

"We're divided in opinion about that," said the girl. "Ingua and I both believe Mr. Cragg murdered him, but Josie isn't sure of it. If he did, however, Josie thinks we will find the poor man's grave somewhere under the stones of the river bed. There was no grave dug on our grounds, that is certain."

Colonel Hathaway regarded her seriously.

"I am sorry, Mary Louise," he remarked, "that we ever decided to mix in this affair. I did not realize, when first you proposed having Josie here, that the thing might become so tragic."

"It has developed under investigation, you see," she replied. "But I am not very sure of Josie's ability, because she is not very sure of it herself. She dare not, even yet, advance a positive opinion. Unless she learned something last night she is still groping in the dark."

"We must give her time," said the Colonel.

"We have accomplished some good, however," continued the girl. "Ingua is much happier and more content. She is improving in her speech and manners and is growing ambitious to become a respectable and refined young lady. She doesn't often give way to temper, as she used to do on every occasion, and I am sure if she could be removed from her grandfather's evil influence she would soon develop in a way to surprise us all."

"Does her grandfather's influence seem to be evil, then?" asked the Colonel.

"He has surrounded her with privations, if not with actual want," said she. "Only the night before last he was in such a violent rage that he tried to smash everything in the house. That is surely an evil example to set before the child, who has a temper of her own, perhaps inherited from him. He has, however, bought her a new dress—the first one she has had in more than a year—so perhaps the old man at times relents toward his granddaughter and tries to atone for his shortcomings."

Gran'pa Jim was thoughtful for a time.

"Perhaps," he presently remarked, "Mr. Cragg has but little money to buy dresses with. I do not imagine that a man so well educated as you report him to be would prefer to live in a hovel, if he could afford anything better."

"If he is now poor, what has he done with all his money?" demanded Mary Louise.

"That is a part of the mystery, isn't it? Do you know, my dear, I can't help having a kindly thought for this poor man; perhaps because he is a grandfather and has a granddaughter —just as I have."

"He doesn't treat her in the same way, Gran'pa Jim," said she, with a loving look toward the handsome old Colonel.

"And there is a perceptible difference between Ingua and Mary Louise," he added with a smile.

They were to have Ingua's dress fitted by Miss Huckins that morning, and as Josie was fast asleep Mary Louise went across to the cottage to go with the girl on her errand. To her surprise she found old Mr. Cragg sitting upon his little front porch, quite motionless and with his arms folded across his chest. He stared straight ahead and was evidently in deep thought. This was odd, because he was usually at his office an hour or more before this time.

Mary Louise hesitated whether to advance or retreat. She had never as yet come into personal contact with Ingua's grandfather and, suspecting him of many crimes, she shrank from meeting him now. But she was herself in plain sight before she discovered his presence and it would be fully as embarrassing to run away as to face him boldly. Moreover, through the open doorway she could see Ingua passing back and forth in the kitchen, engaged in her customary house-work. So on she came.

Mr. Cragg had not seemed to observe her, at first, but as she now approached the porch he rose from his chair and bowed with a courtly grace that astonished her. In many ways his dignified manners seemed to fit his colonial costume.

"You will find Ingua inside, I believe," he said.

"I—I am Mary Louise Burrows."

Again he bowed.

"I am glad to meet you, Miss Burrows. And I am glad that you and Ingua are getting acquainted," he rejoined, in even, well modulated tones. "She has not many friends and her association with you will be sure to benefit her."

Mary Louise was so amazed that she fairly gasped.

"I—I like Ingua," she said. "We're going into town to have her new dress tried on this morning."

He nodded and resumed his chair. His unexpected politeness gave her courage.

"It's going to be a pretty dress," she continued, "and, if only she had a new hat to go with it, Ingua would have a nice outfit. She needs new shoes, though," as an afterthought, "and perhaps a few other little things—like stockings and underwear."

He was silent, wholly unresponsive to her suggestion.

"I—I'd like to buy them for her myself," went on the girl, in a wistful tone, "only Ingua is so proud that she won't accept gifts from me."

Still he remained silent.

"I wonder," she said, with obvious hesitation, "if you would

Edith Van Dyne

allow me to give *you* the things, sir, and then you give them to Ingua, as if they came from yourself."

"No!" It was a veritable explosion, so fierce that she started back in terror. Then he rose from his chair, abruptly quitted the porch and walked down the path toward the bridge in his accustomed deliberate, dignified manner.

Ingua, overhearing his ejaculation, came to the open window to see what had caused it.

"Oh, it's you, Mary Louise, is it?" she exclaimed. "Thank goodness, you've drove Gran'dad off to the office. I thought he'd planted himself in that chair for the whole day."

"Are you ready to go to Miss Huckins'?" asked Mary Louise.

"I will be, in a few minutes. Gran'dad was late gett'n' up this mornin' and that put things back. He had the 'wakes' ag'in last night."

"Oh; did he walk out, then?"

"Got back at about daylight and went to bed. That's why he slep' so late."

Mary Louise reflected that in such a case Josie ought to have some news to tell her. She answered Ingua's inquiries after Josie by saying she was engaged this morning and would not go to town with them, so presently the two girls set off together. Mary Louise was much better qualified to direct the making of the new dress than was Josie, and she gave Miss Huckins some hints on modern attire that somewhat astonished the country dressmaker but were gratefully received. There was no question but that Mary Louise was stylishly, if simply, dressed on all occasions, and so Miss

Huckins was glad to follow the young girl's advice.

They were in the dressmaker's shop a long time, fitting and planning, and when at length they came down the stairs they saw Sol Jerrems standing in his door and closely scrutinizing through his big horn spectacles something he held in his hand. As Mary Louise wished to make a slight purchase at the store she approached the proprietor, who said in a puzzled tone of voice:

"I dunno what t' say to you folks, 'cause I'm up in the air. This money may be genooine, but it looks to me like a counterfeit," and he held up a new ten-dollar bill.

"I want a roll of tape, please," said Mary Louise. "I hope your money is good, Mr. Jerrems, but its value cannot interest us."

"I dunno 'bout that," he replied, looking hard at Ingua, "Ol' Swallertail gimme this bill, not ten minutes ago, an' said as his gran'darter was to buy whatever she liked, as fur as the money would go. That order was so queer that it made me suspicious. See here: a few days ago ol' Cragg bought Ingua a dress—an' paid for it, by gum!—an' now he wants her t' git ten dollars' wuth o' shoes an' things! Don't that look mighty strange?"

"Why?" asked Mary Louise.

"'Cause it's the first money he's spent on the kid since I kin remember, an' he's allus talkin' poverty an' says how he'll die in the poorhouse if prices keep goin' up, as they hev durin' the furrin war that's now hummin' acrost the water. If he's *that* poor, an' on a sudden springs a ten-dollar bill on me for fixin's fer his kid, there's sure somethin' wrong somewhere. I got stuck on a bill jus' like this a year ago, an' I ain't goin' to let any goods go till I find out for sure whether it's real money or not."

"When can you find out?" inquired Mary Louise.

"To-morrer there's a drummer due here f'm the city—a feller keen as a razor—who'll know in a minute if the bill is a counterfeit. If he says it's good, then Ingua kin trade it out, but I ain't goin' to take no chances."

Ingua came close to the storekeeper, her face dark with passion.

"Come," said Mary Louise, taking the child's arm, "let us go home. I am sure Mr. Jerrems is over particular and that the money is all right. But we can wait until to-morrow, easily. Come, Ingua."

The child went reluctantly, much preferring to vent her indignation on old Sol. Mary Louise tried to get her mind off the insult.

"We'll have the things, all right, Ingua," she said. "Wasn't it splendid in your grandfather to be so generous, when he has so little money to spend? And the ten dollars will fit you up famously. I wish, though," she added, "there was another or a better store at the Crossing at which to trade."

"Well, there ain't," observed Ingua, "so we hev to put up with that Sol Jerrems. When I tell Gran'dad about this business I bet he'll punch Sol Jerrems' nose."

"Don't tell him," advised Mary Louise.

"Why not?"

"I think he gave this money to Mr. Jerrems on a sudden impulse. Perhaps, if there is any question about its being genuine, he will take it back, and you will lose the value of it. Better wait until to-morrow, when of course the drummer will pronounce it all right. My opinion is that Mr. Jerrems is so unused to new ten dollar bills that having one makes him unjustly suspicious."

"I guess yer right," said Ingua more cheerfully. "It's amazin' that Gran'dad loosened up at all. An' he might repent, like you say, an' take the money back. So I'll be like ol' Sol—I'll take no chances."

CHAPTER XIX

GOOD MONEY FOR BAD

At luncheon Josie appeared at the table, fresh as ever, and Mary Louise began to relate to her and to her grandfather the occurrences of the morning. When she came to tell how Sol Jerrems had declared the money counterfeit, Josie suddenly sprang up and swung her napkin around her head, shouting gleefully:

"Glory hallelujah! I've got him. I've trapped Old Swallowtail at last."

They looked at her in amazement.

"What do you mean?" asked Mary Louise.

Josie sobered instantly.

"Forgive me," she said; "I'm ashamed of myself. Go on with the story. What became of that counterfeit bill?"

"Mr. Jerrems has it yet. He is keeping it to show to a commercial traveler, who is to visit his store to-morrow. If the man declares the money is good, then Ingua may buy her things."

"We won't bother the commercial traveler," said Josie, in a tone of relief. "I'm going straight down to the store to redeem that bill. I want it in my possession."

Colonel Hathaway regarded her gravely.

"I think our female detective, having said so much and having exhibited such remarkable elation, must now explain her discoveries to us more fully," said he.

"I'd rather not, just yet," protested Josie. "But what have I said in my madness, and what did my words imply?"

"From the little I know of this case," replied the Colonel, "I must judge that you believe Mr. Cragg to be a counterfeiter, and that his mysterious business is—to counterfeit. In this out-of-the-way place," he continued, thoughtfully, "such a venture might be carried on for a long time without detection. Yet there is one thing that to me forbids this theory."

"What is that, sir?"

"A counterfeiter must of necessity have confederates, and Mr. Cragg seems quite alone in the conduct of his mysterious business."

Josie smiled quite contentedly. Confederates? Last night's discoveries had proved that Old Swallowtail had two of these, at least.

"Please don't lisp a word of this suspicion at present," she warned her friends. "If I am right—and I have no doubt of that—we are about to uncover a far-reaching conspiracy to defraud the Government. But the slightest hint of danger would enable them to escape and I want the credit of putting this gang of desperadoes behind the bars. Really, I'd no idea, when I began the investigation, that it would lead to anything so important. I thought, at first, it might be a simple murder case; simple, because the commonest people commit murder, and to the detective the deed is more revolting than exciting. But we may dismiss the murder suspicion entirely."

"Oh, indeed! What about Ned Joselyn's mysterious disappearance?" asked Mary Louise.

"Joselyn? He disappeared for a purpose," answered Josie. "I saw him last night—monocle and all—acting as old Cragg's confederate. Ned Joselyn is one of those I hope to land in prison."

Her hearers seemed quite bewildered by this positive statement.

"Where were you last night?" inquired Mary Louise.

"At that five acres of stones we once visited, which is Mr. Cragg's private property. Hidden somewhere in the hillside is a cavern, and in that cavern the counterfeit money is made. I have heard the printing-press turning it out in quantity; I saw Ned Joselyn come away with a package of the manufactured bills and heard Old Swallowtail implore him to 'play square' with the proceeds. There was another of the gang present, also; a man whom I had considered quite an innocent citizen of Cragg's Crossing until I discovered him with the others. I think it was he who operated the press. It has been a very pretty plot, a cleverly conducted plot; and it has been in successful operation for years. But the gang is in the toils, just now, and little redheaded Josie O'Gorman is going to score a victory that will please her detective daddy mightily." Josie was surely elated when she ventured to boast in this manner. The others were duly impressed.

"You don't mean to arrest those men alone, do you, Josie?" asked the Colonel somewhat anxiously.

"No, indeed. I'm not yet quite ready to spring my trap," she replied. "When the time comes, I must have assistance, but I want to get all my evidence shipshape before I call on the Secret Service to make the capture. I can't afford to bungle so important a thing, you know, and this ten dollar bill, so carelessly given the storekeeper, is going to put one powerful bit of evidence in my hands. That was a bad slip on old Cragg's part, for he has been very cautious in covering his tracks, until now. But I surmise that Mary Louise's pleading for Ingua, this morning, touched his pride, and having no real money at hand he ventured to give the storekeeper a counterfeit. And old Sol, having been caught by a counterfeit once before—I wonder if Old Swallowtail gave him that one, too?—became suspicious of the newness of the bill and so played directly into our hands. So now, if you'll excuse me, I'll run to town without further delay. I won't rest easy until that bill is in my possession."

"I'll go with you," said Mary Louise eagerly.

Half an hour later the two girls entered the store and found the proprietor alone. Mary Louise made a slight purchase, as an excuse, and then Josie laid ten silver dollars on the counter and said carelessly:

"Will you give me a ten dollar bill for this silver, Mr. Jerrems? I want to send it away in a letter."

"Sure; I'd ruther hev the change than the bill," he answered, taking out his wallet. "But I wouldn't send so much money in a letter, if I was you. Better buy a post-office order."

"I know my business," she pertly replied, watching him

unroll the leather wallet. "No; don't give me that old bill. I'd rather have the new one on top."

"That new one," said he, "I don't b'lieve is good. Looks like a counterfeit, to me."

"Let's see it," proposed Josie, taking the bill in her hand and scrutinizing it. "I can tell a counterfeit a mile away. No; this is all right; I'll take it," she decided.

"Yer like to git stung, if ye do," he warned her.

"I'll take my chances," said Josie, folding the bill and putting it in her purse. "You've got good money for it, anyhow, so you've no kick coming, that I can see."

"Why, that must be the bill Mr. Cragg gave you," Mary Louise said to the storekeeper, as if she had just recognized it.

"It is," admitted Sol.

"Then Ingua can now buy her outfit?"

"Any time she likes," he said. "But I want it reg'lar understood that the sewin'-girl can't bring the money back to me, if she finds it bad. I ain't sure it's bad, ye know, but I've warned her, an' now it's her look-out."

"Of course it is," agreed Josie. "But don't worry. The bill is good as gold. I wish I had a hundred like it."

On their way home Josie stopped to call on Ingua, while Mary Louise, at her friend's request, went on.

"I've two important things to tell you," Josie announced to

the child. "One is that you needn't worry any more about Ned Joselyn's being dead. A girl whom I know well has lately seen him alive and in good health, so whatever your grandfather's crimes may have been he is not a murderer."

Ingua was astounded. After a moment she gasped out:

"How d'ye know? Who was the girl? Are ye sure it were Ned Joselyn?"

"Quite sure. He has probably been in hiding, for some reason. But you mustn't tell a soul about this, Ingua; especially your grandfather. It is part of the secret between us, and that's the reason I have told you."

Ingua still stared as if bewildered.

"Who was the girl?" she whispered.

"I can't tell you her name, but you may depend upon the truth of her statement, just the same."

"And she's *sure* it were Ned Joselyn she saw?"

"Isn't he tall and thin, with a light moustache and curly hair, and doesn't he wear a glass in one eye?"

"With a string to it; yes! That's him, sure enough. Where'd she see him?"

"Don't ask me questions. It's a part of the girl's secret, you know. She let me tell you this much, so that you wouldn't worry any longer over the horror of that winter night when your grandfather went to the Kenton house and Joselyn disappeared. I think, Ingua, that the man is crooked, and mixed up with a lot of scoundrels who ought to be in jail."

Edith Van Dyne

Ingua nodded her head.

"Gran'dad told him he was crooked," she affirmed. "I don't say as Gran'dad is a saint, Josie, but he ain't crooked, like Ned—ye kin bank on that—'cause he's a Cragg, an' the Craggs is square-toes even when they're chill'ins."

Josie smiled at this quaint speech. She was sorry for poor Ingua, whose stalwart belief in the Cragg honesty was doomed to utter annihilation when her grandsire was proved to have defrauded the Government by making counterfeit money. But this was no time to undeceive the child, so she said:

"The other bit of news is that Sol Jerrems has traded the bill which he thought was bad for good money, so you can buy your things any time you please."

"Then it wasn't counterfeit?"

"I saw it myself. I've lived in the city so long that no one can fool me with counterfeit money. I can tell it in two looks, Ingua. So I'd rather have a nice new bill than ten clumsy silver dollars and I made the trade myself."

"Where'd ye get so much money, Josie?"

"My wages. I don't do much work, but I get paid regularly once a week."

She didn't explain that her father made her a weekly allowance, but Ingua was satisfied.

"What do you think I orter buy with that money, Josie? I need so many things that it's hard to tell where to begin and where to leave off."

"Let's make a list, then, and figure it out."

This occupied them some time and proved a very fascinating occupation to the poor girl, who had never before had so much money to spend at one time.

"I owe it all to Mary Louise," she said gratefully, as Josie rose to depart. "It seems like no one can refuse Mary Louise anything. When she asked me to be more careful in my speech didn't I do better? I slips, now an' then, but I'ms always tryin'. And she tackled Gran'dad. If you or me—or I—had asked Gran'dad for that money, Josie, we'd never 'a' got it in a thousan' years. Why do you s'pose Mary Louise gits into people the way she does?"

"It's personality, I suppose," answered Josie, thoughtfully. And then, realizing that Ingua might not understand that remark, she added: "There's no sham about Mary Louise; she's so simple and sweet that she wins hearts without any effort. You and I have natures so positive, on the contrary, that we seem always on the aggressive, and that makes folks hold aloof from us, or even oppose us."

"I wish I was like Mary Louise," said Ingua with a sigh.

"I don't," declared Josie. "We can't all be alike, you know, and I'd rather push ahead, and get a few knocks on the way, then have a clear path and no opposition."

Edith Van Dyne

CHAPTER XX

AN UNEXPECTED APPEARANCE

For a week it was very quiet at Cragg's Crossing. The only ripple of excitement was caused by the purchase of Ingua's new outfit. In this the child was ably assisted by Mary Louise and Josie; indeed, finding the younger girl so ignorant of prices, and even of her own needs, the two elder ones entered into a conspiracy with old Sol and slyly added another ten dollars to Ingua's credit. The result was that she carried home not only shoes and a new hat—trimmed by Miss Huckins without cost, the material being furnished from the fund—but a liberal supply of underwear, ribbons, collars and hosiery, and even a pair of silk gloves, which delighted the child's heart more than anything else.

Miss Huckins' new dress proved very pretty and becoming, and with all her wealth of apparel Ingua was persuaded to dine with Mary Louise at the Kenton house on Saturday evening. The hour was set for seven o'clock, in order to allow the girl to prepare her grandfather's supper before going out, and the first intimation Old Swallowtail had of the arrangement was when he entered the house Saturday evening and found Ingua arrayed in all her finery.

He made no remark at first, but looked at her more than

once—whether approvingly or not his stolid expression did not betray. When the girl did not sit down to the table and he observed she had set no place for herself, he suddenly said:

"Well?"

"I'm goin' to eat with the Hathaways to-night," she replied. "Their dinner ain't ready till seven o'clock, so if ye hurry a little I kin wash the dishes afore I go."

He offered no objection. Indeed, he said nothing at all until he had finished his simple meal. Then, as she cleared the table, he said:

"It might be well, while you are in the society of Mary Louise and Colonel Hathaway, to notice their method of speech and try to imitate it."

"What's wrong with my talk?" she demanded. She was annoyed at the suggestion, because she had been earnestly trying to imitate Mary Louise's speech.

"I will leave you to make the discovery yourself," he said dryly.

She tossed her dishes into the hot water rather recklessly.

"If I orter talk diff'rent," said she, "it's your fault. Ye hain't give me no schooling ner noth'n'. Ye don't even say six words a week to me. I'm just your slave, to make yer bed an' cook yer meals an' wash yer dishes. Gee! how'd ye s'pose I'd talk? Like a lady?"

"I think," he quietly responded, "you picked up your slang from your mother, who, however, had some education. The education ruined her for the quiet life here and she plunged

Edith Van Dyne

into the world to get the excitement she craved. Hasn't she been sorry for it many times, Ingua?"

"I don't know much 'bout Marm, an' I don't care whether she's sorry or not. But I do know I need an eddication. If Mary Louise hadn't had no eddication she'd 'a' been just like me: a bit o' junk on a scrap-heap, that ain't no good to itself ner anybody else."

He mused silently for a while, getting up finally and walking over to the door.

"Your peculiarities of expression," he then remarked, as if more to himself than to the child, "are those we notice in Sol Jerrems and Joe Brennan and Mary Ann Hopper. They are characteristic, of the rural population, which, having no spur to improve its vocabulary, naturally grows degenerate in speech."

She glanced at him half defiantly, not sure whether he was "pokin' fun at her" or not.

"If you mean I talks country talk," said she, "you're right. Why shouldn't I, with no one to tell me better?"

Again he mused. His mood was gentle this evening.

"I realize I have neglected you," he presently said. "You were thrust upon me like a stray kitten, which one does not want but cannot well reject. Your mother has not supplied me with money for your education, although she has regularly paid for your keep."

"She has?" cried Ingua, astounded. "Then you've swindled her an' me both, for I pays for more'n my keep in hard work. My keep? For the love o' Mike, what does my keep amount to? A cent a year?"

He winced a little at her sarcasm but soon collected himself. Strangely enough, he did not appear to be angry with her.

"I've neglected you," he repeated, "but it has been an oversight. I have had so much on my mind that I scarcely realized you were here. I forgot you are Nan's child and that you—you needed attention."

Ingua put on her new hat, looking into a cracked mirror.

"Ye might 'a' remembered I'm a Cragg, anyhow," said she, mollified by his tone of self reproach. "An' ye might 'a' remembered as *you're* a Cragg. The Craggs orter help each other, 'cause all the world's ag'in 'em."

He gave her an odd look, in which pride, perplexity and astonishment mingled.

"And you are going into the enemy's camp to-night?"

"Oh, Mary Louise is all right. She ain't like them other snippy girls that sometimes comes here to the big houses. *She* don't care if I *am* a Cragg, or if I talks country. I like Mary Louise."

When she had gone the old man sat in deep thought for a long time. The summer evening cast shadows; twilight fell; darkness gradually shrouded the bare little room. Still he sat in his chair, staring straight ahead into the gloom and thinking.

Then the door opened. Shifting his eyes he discovered a dim shadow in the opening. Whoever it was stood motionless until a low, clear voice asked sharply:

"Anybody home?"

He got up, then, and shuffled to a shelf, where he felt for a kerosene lamp and lighted it.

"Come in, Nan," he said without turning around, as he stooped over the lamp and adjusted the wick.

The yellow light showed a young woman standing in the doorway, a woman of perhaps thirty-five. She was tall, erect, her features well formed, her eyes bright and searching. Her walking-suit was neat and modish and fitted well her graceful, rounded form. On her arm was a huge basket, which she placed upon a chair as she advanced into the room and closed the door behind her.

"So you've come back," remarked Old Swallowtail, standing before her and regarding her critically.

"A self-evident fact, Dad," she answered lightly, removing her hat. "Where's Ingua?"

"At a dinner party across the river."

"That's good. Is she well?"

"What do you care, Nan, whether she is well or not?"

"If she's at a dinner party I needn't worry. Forgive the foolish question, Dad. Brennan promised to bring my suit case over in the morning. I lugged the basket myself."

"What's in the basket?"

"Food. Unless you've changed your mode of living the cupboard's pretty bare, and this is Saturday night. I can sleep on that heartbreaking husk mattress with Ingua, but I'll be skinned if I eat your salt junk and corn pone. Forewarned is forearmed; I brought my own grub."

As she spoke she hung her hat and coat on some pegs, turned the lamp a little higher and then, pausing with hands on hips, she looked inquisitively at her father.

"You seem pretty husky, for your age," she continued, with a hard little laugh.

"You've been prospering, Nan."

"Yes," sitting in a chair and crossing her legs, "I've found my forte at last. For three years, nearly, I've been employed by the Secret Service Department at Washington."

"Ah."

"I've made good. My record as a woman sleuth is excellent. I make more money in a week—when I'm working—than you do in a year. Unless—" She paused abruptly and gave him a queer look.

"Unless it's true that you're coining money in a way that's not legal."

He stood motionless before her, reading her face. She returned his scrutiny with interest. Neither resumed the conversation for a time. Finally the old man sank back into his chair.

"A female detective," said he, a little bitterly, "is still—a female."

"And likewise a detective. I know more about you, Dad, than

Edith Van Dyne

you think," she asserted, in an easy, composed tone that it seemed impossible to disturb. "You need looking after, just at this juncture, and as I've been granted a vacation I ran up here to look after you."

"In what way, Nan?"

"We'll talk that over later. There isn't much love lost between us, more's the pity. You've always thought more of your infernal 'Cause' than of your daughter. But we're Craggs, both of us, and it's the Cragg custom to stand by the family."

It struck him as curious that Ingua had repeated almost those very words earlier that same evening. He had never taught them the Cragg motto, "Stand Fast," that he could remember, yet both Nan and her child were loyal to the code. Was *he* loyal, too? Had he stood by Nan in the past, and Ingua in the present, as a Cragg should do?

His face was a bit haggard as he sat in his chair and faced his frank-spoken daughter, whose clear eyes did not waver before his questioning gaze.

"I know what you're thinking," said she; "that I've never been much of a daughter to you. Well, neither have you been much of a father to me. Ever since I was born and my unknown mother—lucky soul!—died, you've been obsessed by an idea which, lofty and altruistic as you may have considered it, has rendered you self-centered, cold and inconsiderate of your own flesh and blood. Then there's that devilish temper of yours to contend with. I couldn't stand the life here. I wandered away and goodness knows how I managed to live year after year in a struggle with the world, rather than endure your society and the hardships you thrust upon me. You've always had money, yet not a cent would you devote to your family. You lived like a dog and wanted me to do the same, and I wouldn't. Finally I met a good man and married him. He wasn't rich but he was generous. When he died I was thrown on my own resources again, with a child of my own to look after. Circumstances forced me to leave Ingua with you while I hunted for work. I found it. I'm a detective, well-known and respected in my profession."

"I'm glad to know you are prosperous," he said gently, as she paused. He made no excuses. He did not contradict her accusations. He waited to hear her out.

"So," said Nan, in a careless, offhand tone, "I've come here to save you. You're in trouble."

"I am not aware of it."

"Very true. If you were, the danger would be less. I've always had to guess at most of your secret life. I knew you were sly and secretive. I didn't know until now that you've been crooked."

He frowned a little but made no retort.

"It doesn't surprise me, however," she continued. "A good many folks are crooked, at times, and the only wonder is that a clever man like you has tripped and allowed himself to fall under suspicion. Suspicion leads to investigation—when it's followed up—and investigation, in such cases, leads to—jail."

He gave a low growl that sounded like the cry of an enraged beast, and gripped the arms of his chair fiercely. Then he rose and paced the room with frantic energy. Nan watched him with a half smile on her face. When he had finally mastered his wrath and became more quiet she said:

Edith Van Dyne

"Don't worry, Dad. I said I have come to save you. It will be fun, after working for the Government so long, to work against it. There's a certain red-headed imp in this neighborhood who is the daughter of our assistant chief, John O'Gorman. Her name is Josie O'Gorman and she's in training for the same profession of which I'm an ornament. I won't sneer at her, for she's clever, in a way, but I'd like to show O'Gorman that Nan Shelley—that's my name in Washington —is a little more clever than his pet. This Josie O'Gorman is staying with the Hathaway family. She's been probing your secret life and business enterprises and has unearthed an important clew in which the department is bound to be interested. So she sent a code telegram to O'Gorman, who left it on his desk long enough for me to decipher and read it. I don't know what the assistant chief will do about it, for I left Washington an hour later and came straight to you. What I do know is that I'm in time to spike Miss Josie's guns, which will give me a great deal of pleasure. She doesn't know I'm your daughter, any more than O'Gorman does, so if the girl sees me here she'll imagine I'm on Government business. But I want to keep out of her way for a time. Do you know the girl, Dad?"

"Yes," he said.

"She's rather clever."

"Yes."

"I think she'd have nabbed you, presently, if I hadn't taken hold of the case so promptly myself. With our start, and the exercise of a grain of intelligence, we can baffle any opposition the girl can bring to bear. Do you wish to run away?"

"No," he growled.

"I'm glad of that. I like the excitement of facing danger boldly. But there's ample time to talk over details. I see you've had your supper, so I'll just fry myself a beefsteak."

She opened her basket and began to prepare a meal. Old Swallowtail sat and watched her. Presently he smiled grimly and Nan never noticed the expression. Perhaps, had she done so, she would have demanded an explanation. He rarely smiled, and certainly his daughter's disclosures were not calculated to excite mirth, or even to amuse.

CHAPTER XXI

A CASE OF NERVES

The "hotel" at the Crossing was not an imposing affair. Indeed, had there not been an "office" in the front room, with a wooden desk in one corner, six chairs and two boxes of sawdust to serve as cuspidors, the building might easily have been mistaken for a private residence. But it stood on the corner opposite the store and had a worn and scarcely legible sign over the front door, calling it a hotel in capital letters.

The Hoppers, who operated the establishment, did an excellent business. On week days the farmers who came to town to trade made it a point to eat one of Silas Hopper's twenty-five cent dinners, famous for at least five miles around for profusion and good cookery. On Sundays—and sometimes on other days—an automobile party, touring the country, would stop at the hotel for a meal, and Mrs. Hopper was accustomed to have a chicken dinner prepared every Sunday in the hope of attracting a stray tourist. There were two guest rooms upstairs that were religiously reserved in case some patron wished to stay overnight, but these instances were rare unless a drummer missed his train and couldn't get away from the Crossing until the next day.

The Sunday following the arrival of Ingua's mother in town

proved a dull day with the Hoppers, who had been compelled to eat their chicken dinner themselves in default of customers. The dishes had been washed and Mary Ann, the daughter of the house, was sitting on the front porch in her Sunday gown and a rocking-chair, when an automobile drove up to the door and a dapper little man alighted. He was very elaborately dressed, with silk hat, patent-leather shoes and a cane setting off his Prince Albert coat and lavender striped trousers. Across his white waistcoat was a heavy gold watch-guard with an enormous locket dangling from it; he had a sparkling pin in his checkered neck-scarf that might be set with diamonds but perhaps wasn't; on his fingers gleamed two or three elaborate rings. He had curly blond hair and a blond moustache and he wore gold-rimmed eyeglasses. Altogether the little man was quite a dandy and radiated prosperity. So, when the driver of the automobile handed out two heavy suit cases and received from the stranger a crisp bill for his services, Mary Ann Hopper realized with exultation that the hotel was to have a guest.

As the car which had brought him rolled away the little man turned, observed Mary Ann, and removing his silt hat bowed low.

"I presume," said he in precise accents, "that this town is that of Cragg's Crossing, and that this building is the hotel. Am I correct in the surmise?"

"I'll call Pa," said Mary Ann, somewhat embarrassed. Drummers she could greet with unconcern, but this important individual was a man of a different sort. His brilliant personality dazzled her.

Mr. Hopper came out in his shirtsleeves, gave one look at his customer and put on his coat.

"Goin' to stay, sir?" he asked.

"For a time, if I like the accommodations," was the reply. "I am in need of perfect quiet. My doctor says I must court tranquility to avoid a nervous breakdown. I do not know your town; I do not know your hotel; I hired a man in the city to drive me until I came to a quiet place. He assured me, on the way, that this is a quiet place."

"I dunno him," said Hopper, "but he didn't put up no bluff. If ye can find a quieter place ner this, outside a graveyard, I'll board ye fer noth'n'."

"I thank you for your assurance, sir. Can you show me to the best room you can place at my disposal?"

"Had dinner?"

"I thank you, yes. I am weary from the long ride. I will lie down for an hour. Then I will take my usual walk. When I return I would like an omelet with mushrooms—I suppose you have no truffles?—for my evening meal."

The landlord grinned and picked up the suit cases.

"We're jest out o' truffles an' we're out o' mushrooms," he said, "but we're long on eggs an' ye can have 'em omeletted or fried or b'iled, as it suits yer fancy. Sophie's best hold is cookin' eggs. Sophie's my wife, ye know, an' there ain't no better cook in seven counties, so the drummers say."

As he spoke he entered the house and led the way up the stairs.

"Thank you; thank you," said the stranger. "I am glad your good wife is an experienced cook. Kindly ask her to spare no expense in preparing my meals. I am willing to pay liberally for what I receive."

"This room, with board," remarked Hopper, setting down the suit cases in the front corner bedchamber, "will cost you a dollar a day, or five dollars a week—if you eat our reg'lar meals. If ye keep callin' fer extrys, I'll hev to charge ye extry."

"Very reasonable; very reasonable, indeed," declared the stranger, taking a roll of bills from his pocket. "As I am at present unknown to you, I beg you to accept this five-dollar bill in advance. And now, if you will bring me a pitcher of ice-water, I will take my needed siesta. My nerves, as you may have observed, are at somewhat of a tension to-day."

"We're out o' ice," remarked the landlord, pocketing the money, "but ye'll find plenty of good cold water at the pump in the back yard. Anything else, sir?"

"I thank you, no. I am not thirsty. Ice-water is not necessary to my happiness. You will pardon me if I ask to be left alone—with my nerves."

Hopper went away chuckling. His wife and Mary Ann were both at the foot of the stairs, lying in wait to question him.

"That feller's as good as a circus," he asserted, taking off his coat again and lighting his corncob pipe. "He's got nerves an' money, an' he's come here to git rid of 'em both."

"Who is he?" demanded Mrs. Hopper.

"By gum, I fergot to ask him. I got thanked fer ev'rything I did an' ev'rything I couldn't do, an' I've got five dollars o' his money in my jeans as a evidence o' good faith. The whole performance sort o' knocked me out."

"No wonder," asserted, his wife sympathetically.

"I'll bet he's some punkins, though," declared Mary Ann, "an' he'll be a godsend to us after a dull week. Only, remember this, if he kicks on the feed he don't git no satisfaction out o' me."

"I don't think he'll kick on anything," said her father. "He wants eggs for his supper, in a omelet."

"He couldn't want anything that's cheaper to make," said Mrs. Hopper. "The hens are layin' fine jus' now."

"When he comes down, make him register," suggested Mary Ann. "If ye don't, we won't know what ter call him."

"I'll call him an easy mark, whatever his name is," said the landlord, grinning at his own attempt at wit.

The stranger kept his room until five o'clock. Then he came down, spick and span, his cane under his arm, upon his hands a pair of bright yellow kid gloves.

"I will now indulge in my walk," said he, addressing the family group in the office. "My nerves are better, but still vibrant. I shall be further restored on my return."

"Jest sign the register," proposed Hopper, pointing to a worn and soiled book spread upon the counter. "Hate to trouble ye, but it's one o' the rules o' my hotel."

"No trouble, thank you; no trouble at all," responded the stranger, and drawing a fountain-pen from his pocket he approached the register and wrote upon the blank page. "I hope there is, nothing to see in your town," he remarked, turning away. "I don't wish to see anything. I merely desire to walk."

"Yer wish'll come true, I guess," said Hopper. "I've lived here over twenty year an' I hain't seen noth'n' yet. But the walkin' is as good as it is anywhere."

"Thank you. I shall return at six o'clock—for the omelet," and he walked away with short, mincing steps that seemed to them all very comical.

Three heads at once bent over the register, on which the stranger had I written in clear, delicate characters: "Lysander Antonius Sinclair, B. N., Boston, Mass."

"I wonder what the 'B. N.' stands for," said Mary Ann Hopper, curiously.

"Bum Nerves, o' course," replied the landlord. "He's got 'em, sure enough."

Edith Van Dyne

CHAPTER XXII

INGUA'S MOTHER

"And how do you like your grandfather? Is he good to you?" asked Mrs. Scammel on Sunday forenoon, as she sat on the porch beside her small daughter. Old Swallowtail did not usually go to his office on Sundays, but kept his room at the cottage and wrote letters. To-day, however, he had wandered down the path and disappeared, and Nan and Ingua were both glad to see him go.

"No," answered the child to both questions.

"You don't like him?"

"How can I, when he jes' sets an' glares at me ev'ry time he comes into the house—'cept when he complains I ain't doin' my work proper? It were a sort o' mean trick o' yours, Marm, leavin' me here to slave fer that ol' man while you was off in the cities, havin' a good time."

"Yes," said Nan, "I was frolicking with starvation until I got a job, and it was the sort of job that wouldn't allow having a child around. But since I've been making money I've sent Dad five dollars every week, for your clothes and board."

"You have?"

"Every week."

"Ten cents a week would pay for all the grub he gives me, an' there ain't a beggar in the county that sports the rags an' tatters I does. That new dress I had on las' night was the first thing in clothes he's bought me for a year, and I guess I wouldn't have had that if Mary Louise hadn't told him he orter dress me more decent."

Nan's brow grew dark.

"I'll have it out with him for that," she promised. "What does he do with his money, Ingua?"

"Salts it, I guess. I never see him have any. It's one o' the mysteries, Marm. Mysteries is thick aroun' Gran'dad, an' folks suspicion 'most anything about him. All I know is that he ain't no spendthrift. Once, when Ned Joselyn used to come here, there was lots of money passed between 'em. I saw it myself. I helped pick it up, once, when they quarreled an' upset the table an' spilled things. But since Ned run ayray. Gran'dad's be'n more savin' than ever."

"Ingua," said Nan, thoughtfully, "I want you to tell me all you know about Ned Joselyn, from the time he first came here."

Ingua regarded her mother with serious eyes.

"All?" she inquired.

"Everything, little or big, that you can recollect."

"You'll stick to Gran'dad, won't ye?"

"That's what I'm here for. There are enemies on his trail and I mean to save him."

"What's he done?"

"I've got to find that out. When I was here before, I knew he had some secret interest to which he was devoted, but I was too indifferent to find out what it was. Now I want to know. If I'm going to save him from the penalties of his crime I must know what the crime is. I think this man Joselyn is mixed up with it in some way, so go ahead and tell me all you know about him."

Ingua obeyed. For more than an hour she earnestly related the story of Ned Joselyn, only pausing to answer an occasional question from her mother. When she came to that final meeting at Christmas week and Joselyn's mysterious disappearance, Nan asked:

"Do you think he killed him?"

"I was pretty sure of it till yest'day, when Josie told me a friend of hers had seen him alive an' well."

"Josie O'Gorman?"

"No, Josie Jessup. She's the sewin'-girl over to Mary Louise's."

"I know; but that girl has more names than one. Do you know her very well, Ingua?"

"She's my best chum," declared the child. "Josie's a dandy girl, an' I like her."

"Have you told her anything about your gran'dad?"

"A little," Ingua admitted, hesitating.

"See here," said Nan, scowling, "I'll put you wise. This red-headed Josie O'Gorman is a detective. She's the daughter of the man I work for in Washington—the assistant chief of the Department—and she is here to try to land your gran'dad in jail. What's more, Ingua, she's likely to do it, unless you and I find a way to head her off."

Ingua's face depicted astonishment, grief, disappointment. Finally she said:

"Gran'dad didn't murder Ned, for Josie herself told me so; so I can't see what he's done to go to jail for."

"He has counterfeited money," said Nan in a low voice.

"Gran'dad has?"

"So they say, and I believe it may be true. Josie has wired her father that she's got the goods on Old Swallowtail and has asked that somebody be sent to arrest him. I saw the telegram and made up my mind I'd get the start of the O'Gormans. Dad won't run away. I've warned him they are on his trail and he didn't make any reply. But I wouldn't be surprised if he's gone, this very day, to cover up his traces. He's bright enough to know that if he destroys all evidence they can't prove anything against him."

She spoke musingly, more to herself than the child beside her, but Ingua drew a deep sigh and remarked:

"Then it's all right. Gran'dad is slick. They'll hev to get up early in the mornin' to beat him at his own game. But I wonder what he does with the counterfeit money, or the real money he trades it for."

"I think I know," said her mother. "He's chucked a fortune into one crazy idea, in which his life has been bound up ever since I can remember, and I suppose he tried counterfeiting to get more money to chuck away in the same foolish manner."

"What crazy idea is that?" inquired Ingua.

"I'll tell you, sometime. Just now I see your friend Josie coming, and that's a bit of good luck. I'm anxious to meet her, but if she sees me first she won't come on." As she spoke she rose swiftly and disappeared into the house. "Stay where you are, Ingua," she called from within in a low voice; "I don't want her to escape."

Josie was even now making her way across the stepping-stones. Presently she ran up the bank, smiling, and plumped down beside Ingua.

"Top o' the morning to you," said she. "How did you enjoy your first evening in society?"

"They were all very good to me," replied Ingua slowly, looking at her friend with troubled eyes. "I had a nice time, but—"

"You were a little shy," said Josie, "but that was only natural. When you get better acquainted with Mary Louise and the dear old Colonel, you'll—"

She stopped abruptly, for looking up she saw standing in the doorway Nan Shelley—by which name she knew her—who was calmly regarding her. The shock of surprise, for shock it surely was, seemed brief, for almost instantly Josie completed her broken speech:

"When you know them better you'll feel quite at home in their society. Hello, Nan."

"What! Josie O'Gorman? You here?" with well-affected surprise.

"You know it. But how came *you* here, Nan? Has Daddy sent you to help me?"

"Help you! In what way?"

"Help me enjoy country life," said Josie, coloring at her slip.

"Why, I'm on a vacation. You don't seem to understand. I'm—Ingua's mother."

Josie's self-control wasn't proof against this second shock. Her blue eyes stared amazed. With a low exclamation she stood up and faced the woman.

"Ingua's mother! You, Nan?"

"Just so," with a quiet smile.

"Then you ought to be ashamed of yourself," declared Josie with righteous indignation. "You're one of the best paid women in the Department, and you've left your poor child here to starve and slave for a wretched old—," she paused.

"Well, what is he?" asked Nan with tantalizing gentleness.

"An old skinflint, at the least. Shame on you, Nan! Ingua is a dear little girl, and you—you're an unnatural mother. Why, I never suspected you were even married."

"I'm a widow, Josie."

Edith Van Dyne

"And Old Swallowtail is your father? How strange. But— why did you come here just now?" with sudden suspicion.

"I've just finished the Hillyard case and they gave me a vacation. So I came here to see my little girl. I didn't know she was being neglected, Josie. I shall take better care of her after this. My visit to Cragg's Crossing is perfectly natural, for I was born here. But you? What are you up to, Josie?"

"I'm visiting Mary Louise Burrows."

"With what object?"

A detective must be quick-witted. Josie's brain was working with lightning-like rapidity. In a few brief seconds she comprehended that if Nan was Old Swallowtail's daughter, home on a vacation, she must not be allowed to know that Josie was conducting a case against her father. Otherwise she might interfere and spoil everything. She knew Nan of old and respected her keen intelligence. Once, when they had been pitted against each other, Josie had won; but she was not sure she could defeat Nan a second time. Therefore it was imperative that old Cragg's daughter remain in ignorance of the fact that Josie was awaiting reinforcements from Washington in order to arrest Nan's father as a counterfeiter. Also Josie realized instantly that Ingua was likely to tell her mother all she knew about Joselyn, including the story she had told Josie; so, without hesitation she answered Nan's question with apparent frankness:

"Really, Nan, I came here on a wild-goose chase. A man named Ned Joselyn had mysteriously disappeared and his wife feared he had met with foul play. I traced him to this place and as Colonel Hathaway and Mary Louise were living here—in Mrs. Joselyn's own house, by the way—I had myself invited as their guest. Well, the long and short of it is that Joselyn isn't murdered, after all. He simply skipped, and since I came here to worry my poor brain over the fellow he has been discovered, still in hiding but very much alive."

"You suspected my father of killing him?"

"I did; and so did others; but it seems he didn't. But, even with that precious bubble burst, Mary Louise insists on my staying for a visit; so here I am, and your little girl has become my friend."

Ingua knew this story to be quite correct, as far as it regarded her grandfather and Ned Joselyn. Its straightforward relation renewed her confidence in Josie. But Nan knew more than Josie thought she did, having intercepted the girl's telegram to her father; so she said with a slight sneer which she took no pains to conceal:

"You're a clever girl, Josie O'Gorman; a mighty clever girl. You're so clever that I wouldn't be surprised if it tripped you, some day, and landed you on your pug nose."

Which proved that Nan was *not* clever, for Josie's indulgent smile masked the thought: "She knows all and is here to defend her father. I must look out for Nan, for she has a notion I'm still on the track of Hezekiah Cragg."

Edith Van Dyne

CHAPTER XXIII

PECULIAR PEOPLE

Old Swallowtail came home at about four o'clock in the afternoon. The day was hot, yet the old man seemed neither heated nor wearied. Without a word to his daughter or Ingua he drew a chair to the little shady porch and sat down in their company. Nan was mending her child's old frock; Ingua sat thinking.

For half an hour, perhaps, silence was maintained by all. Then Nan turned and asked:

"Have you covered your tracks?"

He turned his glassy, expressionless eyes toward her.

"My tracks, as you call them," said he, "have been laid for forty years or more. They are now ruts. I cannot obliterate them in a day."

The woman studied his face thoughtfully.

"You are not worrying over your probable arrest?"

"No."

"Then it's all right," said she, relieved. "You're a foxy old rascal, Dad, and you've held your own for a good many years. I guess you don't need more than a word of warning."

He made no reply, his eyes wandering along the path to the bridge. Mary Louise was coming their way, walking briskly. Her steps slowed a bit as she drew nearer, but she said in an eager voice:

"Oh, Mrs. Scammel, Josie has told me you are here and who you are. Isn't it queer how lives get tangled up? But I remember you with gratitude and kindliest thoughts, because you were so considerate of my dear Gran'pa Jim. And to think that you are really Ingua's mother!"

Nan rose and took the girl's hands in her own.

"I fear I've been a bad mother to my kid," she replied, "but I thought she was all right with her grandfather and happy here. I shall look after her better in the future."

Mary Louise bowed to Mr. Cragg, who nodded his head in acknowledgment. Then she sat down beside Ingua.

"Are you plannin' to take me away from here, Mama?" asked the child.

"Wouldn't you rather be with me than with your grand-father?" returned Nan with a smile.

"I dunno," said Ingua seriously. "You're a detective, an' I don't like detections. You ain't much like a mother to me, neither, ner I don't know much about you. I dunno yet whether I'm goin' to like you or not."

A wave of color swept over Nan's face; Mary Louise was

shocked; the old man turned his inscrutable gaze down the path once more.

"I like it here," continued the child, musingly: "Gran'dad makes me work, but he don't bother me none 'cept when the devils get, hold o' him. I 'member that you git the devils, too, once in awhile, Marm, an' they're about as fierce as Gran'dad's is. An' I gets 'em 'cause I'm a Cragg like the rest o' you, an' devils seem to be in the Cragg blood. I've a notion it's easier to stand the devils in the country here, than in the city where you live."

Nan didn't know whether to be amused or angry.

"Yet you tried to run away once," she reminded Ingua, "and it was Mary Louise who stopped you. You told me of this only an hour ago.

"Didn't I say the devils pick on *me* sometimes?" demanded the girl. "An' Mary Louise was right. She fought the devils for me, and I'm glad she did, 'cause I've had a good time with her ever since," and she pressed Mary Louise's hand gratefully.

Her child's frankness was indeed humiliating to Nan Scammel, who was by no means a bad woman at heart and longed to win the love and respect of her little girl. Ingua's frank speech had also disturbed Mary Louise, and made her sorry for both the child and her mother. Old Swallowtail's eyes lingered a moment on Ingua's ingenuous countenance but he exhibited no emotion whatever.

"You're a simple little innocent," remarked Nan to Ingua, after a strained pause. "You know so little of the world that your judgment is wholly unformed. I've a notion to take you to Washington and buy you a nice outfit of clothes—like those of Mary Louise, you know—and put you into a first-class girls' boarding-school. Then you'll get civilized, and perhaps amount to something."

"I'd like that," said Ingua, with a first display of enthusiasm; "but who'd look after Gran'dad?"

"Why, we must provide for Dad in some way, of course," admitted Nan after another pause. "I can afford to hire a woman to keep house for him, if I hold my present job. I suppose he has a hoard of money hidden somewhere, but that's no reason he wouldn't neglect himself and starve if left alone. And, if he's really poor, I'm the one to help him. How does that arrangement strike you, Ingua?"

"It sounds fine," replied the girl, "but any woman that'd come *here* to work, an' would stan' Gran'dad's devils, wouldn't amount to much, nohow. If we're goin' to move to the city," she added with a sigh, "let's take Gran'dad with us."

This conversation was becoming too personal for Mary Louise to endure longer. They talked of Mr. Cragg just as if he were not present, ignoring him as he ignored them. With an embarrassed air Mary Louise rose.

"I must go now," said she. "I just ran over to welcome you, Mrs. Scammel, and to ask you and Ingua to dine with us to-morrow night. Will you come? Josie O'Gorman is with us, you know, and I believe you are old friends."

Nan hesitated a moment.

"Thank you," she replied, "we'll be glad to come. You've been mighty good to my little girl and I am grateful. Please give my regards to Colonel Hathaway."

When Mary Louise had gone the three lapsed into silence again. Ingua was considering, in her childish but practical way, the proposed changes in her life. The mother was trying to conquer her annoyance at the child's lack of filial affection, tacitly admitting that the blame was not Ingua's. The old man stared at the path. Whatever his thoughts might be he displayed no hint of their nature.

Presently there appeared at the head of the path, by the bridge, the form of a stranger, a little man who came on with nervous, mincing steps. He was dressed in dandified fashion, with tall silk hat, a gold-headed cane and yellow kid gloves. Almost had he reached the porch when suddenly he stopped short, looked around in surprise and ejaculated:

"Bless me—bless me! I—I've made a mistake. This is a private path to your house. No thoroughfare. Dear me, what an error; an unpardonable error. I hope you will excuse me— I—I hope so!"

"To be sure we will," replied Nan with a laugh, curiously eyeing the dapper little man. "The only way out, sir, is back by the bridge."

"Thank you. Thank you very much," he said earnestly. "I—I am indulging in a stroll and—and my mind wandered, as did my feet. I—I am an invalid in search of rest. Thank you. Good afternoon."

He turned around and with the same mincing, regular steps retreated along the path. At the bridge he halted as if undecided, but finally continued along the country road past the Kenton Place.

Ingua laughed delightedly at the queer man. Nan smiled. Old Swallowtail had altered neither his position nor his blank expression.

"He's a queer fish, ain't he?" remarked the girl. "He's pretty lively for an invalid what's lookin' for rest. I wonder when he landed, an' where he's stoppin'."

Something in the child's remark made Nan thoughtful. Presently she laid down her work and said:

"I believe I'll take a little walk, myself, before dark. Want to go along, Ingua?"

Ingua was ready. She had on her new dress and hoped they might meet someone whom she knew. They wandered toward the town, where most of the inhabitants were sitting outf of doors—a Sunday afternoon custom. Jim Bennett, in his shirtsleeves, was reading a newspaper in front of the postoffice; Sol Jerrems and his entire family occupied the platform before the store, which was of course locked; Nance Milliker was playing the organ in the brown house around the corner, and in front of the hotel sat Mary Ann Hopper in her rocking-chair.

Nan strolled the length of the street, startling those natives who had formerly known her, Ingua nodded and smiled at everyone. Mary Ann Hopper called, as they passed her: "Hullo, Ingua. Where'd ye git the new duds?"

"Miss Huckins made 'em," answered Ingua proudly.

"I guess I'll go and shake hands with Mrs. Hopper," said Nan. "Don't you remember me, Mary Ann? I'm Nan Cragg."

"Gee! so y'are," exclaimed Mary Ann wonderingly. "We all 'spicioned you was dead, long ago."

Edith Van Dyne

"I'm home for a visit. You folks seem prosperous. How's business?"

"Pretty good. We got a new boarder to-day, a feller with bum nerves who come from the city. Gee! but he's togged out t' kill. Got money, too, an' ain't afraid to spend it. He paid Dad in advance."

"That's nice," said Nan. "What's his name?"

"It's a funny name, but I can't remember it. Ye kin see it on the register."

Nan went inside, leaving Ingua with Mary Ann, and studied the name on the register long and closely.

"No," she finally decided, "Lysander isn't calculated to arouse suspicion. He wears a wig, I know, but that is doubtless due to vanity and not a disguise. I at first imagined it was someone O'Gorman had sent down here to help Josie, but none of our boys would undertake such a spectacular personation, bound to attract attention. This fellow will become the laughing-stock of the whole town and every move he makes will be observed. I'm quite sure there is nothing dangerous in the appearance here of Mr. Lysander Antonius Sinclair."

She chatted a few minutes with Mrs. Hopper, whom she found in the kitchen, and then she rejoined Ingua and started homeward. Scarcely were mother and child out of sight when Mr. Sinclair came mincing along from an opposite direction and entered the hotel. He went to his room but soon came down and in a querulous voice demanded his omelet, thanking the landlady again and again for promising it in ten minutes.

He amused them all very much, stating that an omelet for an evening meal was "an effective corrective of tired nerves" and would enable him to sleep soundly all night.

"I sleep a great deal," he announced after he had finished his supper and joined Mr. Hopper on the porch. "When I have smoked a cigar—in which luxury I hope you will join me, sir—I shall retire to my couch and rest in the arms of Morpheus until the brilliant sun of another day floods the countryside."

"P'r'aps it'll rain," suggested the landlord.

"Then Nature's tears will render us sweetly sympathetic."

He offered his cigar case to Mr. Hopper, who recognized a high priced cigar and helped himself.

"Didn't see anything to make ye nervous, durin' yer walk, did ye?" he inquired, lighting the weed.

"Very little. It seems a nice, quiet place. Only once was I annoyed. I stumbled into a private path, just before I reached the river, and—and had to apologize."

"Must 'a' struck Ol' Swallertail's place," remarked the landlord.

"Old Swallowtail? Old Swallowtail? And who is he?" queried the stranger.

Hopper was a born gossip, and if there was any one person he loved to talk of and criticize and "pick to pieces" it was Old Swallowtail. So he rambled on for a half hour, relating the Cragg history in all its details, including the story of Ingua and Ingua's mother, Nan Cragg, who had married some unknown chap named Scammel, who did not long survive the ceremony.

Mr. Sinclair listened quietly, seeming to enjoy his cigar more than he did the Cragg gossip. He asked no questions, letting the landlord ramble on as he would, and finally, when Hopper had exhausted his fund of fact and fiction, which were about evenly mixed, his guest bade him good night and retired to his private room.

"It ain't eight o'clock, yet," said the landlord to his wife, "but a feller with nerves is best asleep. An' when he's asleep he won't waste our kerosene."

No, Mr. Sinclair didn't waste the Hopper kerosene. He had a little pocket arrangement which supplied him with light when, an hour before midnight, he silently rose, dressed himself and prepared to leave the hotel. He was not attired in what Mary Ann called his "glad rags" now, but in a dark gray suit of homespun that was nearly the color of the night. The blond wig was carefully locked in a suit case, a small black cap was drawn over his eyes, and thus—completely transformed—Mr. Hopper's guest had no difficulty in gaining the street without a particle of noise betraying him to the family of his host.

He went to the postoffice, pried open a window, unlocked the mail bag that was ready for Jim Bennett to carry to the morning train at Chargrove and from it abstracted a number of letters which he unsealed and read with great care. They had all been written and posted by Hezekiah Cragg. The man spent a couple of hours here, resealing the envelopes neatly and restoring them to the mail bag, after which, he attached the padlock and replaced the bag in exactly its former position. When he had left the little front room which was devoted by the Bennetts to the mail service, the only evidence of his visit was a bruised depression beside the window-sash which was quite likely to escape detection.

After this the stranger crept through the town and set off at a brisk pace toward the west, taking the road over the bridge and following it to the connecting branch and thence to the lane. A half hour later he was standing in old Cragg's stone lot and another hour was consumed among the huge stones by the hillside—the place where Josie had discovered the entrance to the underground cave. Mr. Sinclair did not discover the entrance, however, so finally he returned to town and mounted the stairs beside Sol Jerrem's store building to the upper hallway.

In five minutes he was inside of Cragg's outer office; in another five minutes he had entered the inner office. There he remained until the unmistakable herald of dawn warned him to be going. However, when he left the building there was no visible evidence of his visit. He was in his own room and in bed long before Mrs. Hopper gave a final snore and wakened to light the kitchen fire and prepare for the duties of the day.

Edith Van Dyne

CHAPTER XXIV

FACING DANGER

Nan's presence at Cragg's Crossing rendered Josie O'Gorman uneasy. She had the Cragg case so well in hand, now, and the evidence in her possession was so positively incriminating, in her judgment, that she did not like to be balked by a clever female detective from her father's own office. She had little doubt but Nan would do all in her power to save old Hezekiah Cragg from the penalty of his misdeeds, and her greatest fear was that he might utterly disappear before O'Gorman sent her assistance.

With this fear growing in her mind, on Monday she determined to send another telegram to her father, urging haste, so she obtained permission from the Colonel to have Uncle Eben drive her and Mary Louise to the city, there being no telegraph office at Chargrove Station. But she timed the trip when no trains would stop at Chargrove during her absence and at the telegraph office she sent an imperative message to John O'Gorman at Washington demanding instant help. Since all counterfeiting cases belonged distinctly to the Secret Service Department she had little doubt her father would respond as soon as the affairs at the office would permit him to do so. But the delay was exasperating, nevertheless. Indeed, Josie was so sure that the crisis of her case was imminent that she determined to watch old Cragg's house every night until his arrest could be made. If he attempted to escape she would arrest him herself, with the aid of the little revolver she carried in her dress pocket.

On their return journey they overtook Mr. Sinclair at about a mile from the Crossing. They had never seen the man before, but when he signaled them. Uncle Eben slowed up the machine and stopped beside him.

"I beg a thousand pardons," said the dapper little stranger, removing his silk hat and bowing profoundly to the two girls, "but would you mind taking me to the town? I—I—fear I have turned my ankle; not seriously, you know, but it is uncomfortable; so if I may sit beside your chauffeur the favor will be greatly appreciated."

"To be sure," said Mary Louise with ready. "Can you get in unaided, or do you wish Uncle Eben to assist you?"

"Thank you; thank you a thousand times, young lady," said he, climbing into the front seat. "I'm stopping at the hotel," he explained, as the car again started, "for rest and quiet, because of my nervous condition. My doctor said I would suffer a nervous breakdown if I did not seek rest and quiet in the seclusion of some country village. So I came here, and—it's secluded; it really is."

"I hope your ankle is not seriously injured, sir," said Mary Louise. "Take the gentleman to the hotel, Uncle Eben."

"Thank you," said the little man, and fussily removing a card-case from an inner pocket he added: "My card, please," and handed it to Mary Louise.

Josie glanced at the card, too. She had been regarding the

stranger thoughtfully, with the same suspicions of him that Nan had formerly entertained. The card was not printed; it was engraved: one point in the man's favor. His blond hair was a wig; she had a good view of the back of it and was not to be deceived. But perhaps the moustache, which matched the hair, was genuine. Carefully considering the matter, she did not think anyone would come to Cragg's Crossing in disguise unless he were a confederate of Hezekiah Cragg, helping to circulate the counterfeit money. This odd Mr. Sinclair might be such a person and working under the direction of Ned Joselyn. Joselyn was in hiding, for some unexplained reason; Sinclair could appear openly. There might be nothing in this supposition but Josie determined to keep an eye on the nervous stranger.

He was profuse in his thanks when they let him out at Hopper's Hotel and Uncle Eben chuckled all the way home.

"Dat man am shuah some mighty 'stravagant punkins, in he's own mind," he remarked. "He oughteh git he's pictur' took in dat outfit, Ma'y Weeze, jes' to show how 'dic'lous a white man can look. He'll have all de kids in town a-chasin' of him, if he gits loose on de streets. All he needs is a brass ban' to be a circus parade."

Nan and Ingua came over to dinner that evening and Josie was very cordial to Ingua's mother, who treated her chief's daughter with the utmost friendliness. Both Ingua and Mary Louise were surprised by their politeness and comradeship, but neither of the principals was deceived by such a display. Each was on her guard, but realized it was wise to appear friendly.

Monday night Josie lurked in the shadows of the river bank until daybreak, never relaxing her espionage of the Cragg house for a moment. All was quiet, however.

Tuesday passed without event. Tuesday night Josie was at her post again, her eyes fixed on the dim light that shone from Mr. Cragg's room. Had she been able to see through the walls of the cottage she would have found the old man seated in his private apartment opposite his daughter. Could she have heard their conversation—the low, continuous hum of Old Swallowtail's voice, broken only by an occasional question from Nan—she would surely have been astonished. Nan was not much astonished, save at the fact that her father had at last voluntarily confided to her the strange story of his life, a life hitherto unknown to her. She was not easily surprised, but she was greatly impressed, and when he finally rose from his chair and went out into the night Nan sat in meditation for some time before she followed him. Ingua had long been asleep.

Josie, lurking outside, had not expected Old Swallowtail to leave the premises unless he planned to run away. His delivery of counterfeit money to Ned Joselyn had been of too recent a date to render it necessary that he revisit his stone-yard for some time to come, she argued; yet to-night, at a little after eleven o'clock, she saw his shadow pass from the house and take the path to the bridge.

Josie followed. At the bridge Mr. Cragg turned westward and at once she surmised he was bound for his rocky five acres. The old man walked deliberately, never thinking to look behind him. He might not have observed anything suspicious had he turned, but a hundred feet behind him came Josie O'Gorman, deftly dodging from tree to bush to keep in the dark places by the wayside. And behind Josie silently moved a little man in gray homespun, whose form it would be difficult to distinguish even while he stood in the open. Josie, like the prey she stalked, was too occupied to look behind.

Old Swallowtail reached the stone-yard and climbed the

fence. While he paused there Josie crept close and noticed a light which suddenly flashed from the hillside. It was a momentary flash and not very brilliant, but she knew it was a signal because the old man at once started forward. She let him lead on until he disappeared among the rocks and then she boldly followed. She knew now where the secret entrance to the cavern was located.

Threading her way cautiously through the maze of rocks the girl finally reached a slanting shelf beneath which she crept on hands and knees. At its farthest edge was a square door of solid oak, rather crudely constructed but thick and substantial. This door stood ajar.

Josie, crouching beside the secret entrance, wondered what she ought to do. The regular thumping, as of machinery, which she had heard once before, now began and continued without interruption. Here was an opportunity to catch the counterfeiters redhanded, but she was one small girl as opposed to a gang of desperate criminals.

"Oh, dear!" she whispered, half aloud, "I wish father had paid some attention to my telegram."

"He did," responded a soft voice beside her.

CHAPTER XXV

FATHER AND DAUGHTER

The girl would have screamed had not a hand been swiftly laid across her lips to stifle the sound. She tried to rise, but the shelf of rock beneath which she crouched prevented her. However, she struggled until an arm was passed firmly around her waist and a stern voice said warningly:

"Josie! Control yourself."

Instantly her form relaxed and became inert. She breathed hard and her heart still raced, but she was no longer afraid.

"Kiss me, Daddy!" she whispered, and the man obeyed with a chuckle of delight.

There was silence for a time, while she collected herself. Then she asked in a businesslike tone:

"When did you get here?"

"Sunday," said he.

"Good gracious! You must have caught the first train after getting my wire."

Edith Van Dyne

"I did. A certain gang of unknown counterfeiters has been puzzling me a good deal lately, and I fancied you had located the rascals."

"I have," said Josie exultantly.

"Where?" he asked.

"The rascals are down below us this very minute, Daddy. They are at our mercy."

"Old Cragg and Jim Bennett?"

"Yes; and perhaps others."

"M-m-m," mumbled O'Gorman, "you've a lot to learn yet, Josie. You're quick; you're persevering; you're courageous. But you lack judgment."

"Do you mean that you doubt my evidence?" she asked indignantly.

"I do."

"I've the counterfeit bill here in my pocket, which Cragg tried to pass on the storekeeper," she said.

"Let me see it."

Josie searched and found the bill. O'Gorman flashed a circle of light on it and studied it attentively.

"Here," he said, passing it back to her. "Don't lose it, Josie. It's worth ten dollars."

"Isn't it counterfeit?" she asked, trying to swallow a big lump that rose in her throat.

"It is one of the recent issues, good as gold."

She sat silent, rigid with disappointment. Never had she been as miserable as at this moment. She felt like crying, and a sob really did become audible in spite of her effort to suppress it. Again O'Gorman passed his arm affectionately around her waist and held her close while she tried to think what it all meant.

"Was that bill your only basis of suspicion, dear?" he presently inquired.

"No, indeed. Do you hear that noise? What are they doing down there?"

"I imagine they are running a printing press," he replied.

"Exactly!" she said triumphantly. "And why do these men operate a printing press in a secret cavern, unless they are printing counterfeit money?"

"Ah, there you have allowed your imagination to jump," returned her father. "Haven't I warned you against the danger of imagination? It leads to theory, and theory leads—nine times in ten—to failure."

"Circumstantial evidence is often valuable," declared Josie.

"It often convicts," he admitted, "but I am never sure of its justice. Whenever facts are obtainable, I prefer facts."

"Can you explain," she said somewhat coldly, for she felt she was suffering a professional rebuke, "what those men below us are printing, if not counterfeit money?"

"I can," said he.

"And you have been down there, investigating?"

"Not yet," he answered coolly.

"Then *you* must be theorizing, Daddy."

"Not at all. If you know you have two marbles in one pocket and two more in another pocket, you may be positive there are four altogether, whether you bother to count them individually or not."

She pondered this, trying to understand what he meant.

"You don't know old Cragg as well as I do," she asserted.

"Let us argue that point," he said quickly. "What do you know about him?"

"I know him to be an eccentric old man, educated and shrewd, with a cruel and murderous temper; I know that he has secluded himself in this half-forgotten town for many years, engaged in some secret occupation which he fears to have discovered. I am sure that he is capable of any crime and therefore—even if that bill is good—I am none the less positive that counterfeiting is his business. No other supposition fits the facts in the case."

"Is that all you know about old Cragg?" asked O'Gorman.

"Isn't it enough to warrant his arrest?" she retorted.

"Not quite. You've forgotten to mention one thing among his characteristics, Josie."

"What is that?"

"Cragg is an Irishman—just as I am."

"What has that to do with it?"

"Only this: his sympathies have always been interested in behalf of his downtrodden countrymen. I won't admit that they *are* downtrodden, Josie, even to you; but Cragg thinks they are. His father was an emigrant and Hezekiah was himself born in Dublin and came to this country while an infant. He imagines he is Irish yet. Perhaps he is."

There was a note of bewilderment in the girl's voice as she asked:

"What has his sympathy for the Irish to do with this case?"

"Hezekiah Cragg," explained O'Gorman, speaking slowly, "is at the head of an organization known as the 'Champions of Irish Liberty.' For many years this C. I. L. fraternity has been growing in numbers and power, fed by money largely supplied by Cragg himself. I have proof, indeed, that he has devoted his entire fortune to this cause, as well as all returns from his business enterprises. He lives in comparative poverty that the Champions of Irish Liberty may finally perfect their plans to free Ireland and allow the Irish to establish a self-governing republic."

"But—why all this secrecy, Daddy?" she asked wonderingly.

"His work here is a violation of neutrality; it is contrary to the treaty between our country and England. According to our laws Hezekiah Cragg and his followers, in seeking to deprive England of her Irish possession, are guilty of treason."

Edith Van Dyne

"Could he be prosecuted for sympathizing with his own race?"

"No; for sending them arms and ammunition to fight with, yes. And that is what they have been doing."

"Then you can arrest him for this act?"

"I can," said O'Gorman, "but I'll be hanged if I will, Josie. Cragg is an idealist; the cause to which he has devoted his life and fortune with a steadfast loyalty that is worthy of respect, is doomed to failure. The man's every thought is concentrated on his futile scheme and to oppose him at this juncture would drive him mad. He isn't doing any real harm to our country and even England won't suffer much through his conspiracy. But, allowing for the folly of his attempt to make his people free and independent, we must admire his lofty philanthropy, his self-sacrifice, his dogged perseverence in promoting the cause so near and dear to his heart. Let some other federal officer arrest him, if he dares; it's no work for an O'Gorman."

Josie had encountered many surprises during her brief career as an embryo detective, but this revelation was the crowning astonishment of her life. All her carefully prepared theories concerning Hezekiah Cragg had been shattered by her father's terse disclosure and instead of hating Old Swallowtail she suddenly found sympathy for his ideals welling in her heart. Josie O 'Gorman was Irish, too.

She pondered deeply the skilled detective's assertions and tried to fit them to her knowledge of old Cragg's character. The story seemed to account for much, but not all. After a time she said:

"But this mysterious business of his, which causes him to

write so many letters and to receive so many answers to them—what connection can it have with the Champions of Irish Liberty?"

"Very little," said her father, "except that it enables Cragg to earn more money to feed into the ever-hungry maw of the Cause. Cragg's 'business' is one of the most unique things of the sort that I have ever encountered. And, while it is quite legitimate, he is obliged to keep it secret so as not to involve his many customers in adverse criticism."

"What on earth can it be?"

"It pertains to heaven, not earth, my dear," said O'Gorman dryly. "Cragg was educated for the ministry or the priesthood —I can't discover whether he was Catholic or Protestant— but it seems he wasn't fitted for the church. Perhaps he already had in mind the idea of devoting his life to the land that gave him birth. Anyhow, he was a well versed theologian, and exceptionally brilliant in theses, so when his money gave out he began writing sermons for others to preach, doing a mail-order business and selling his products to those preachers who are too busy or too lazy to write their own sermons. He has a sort of syndicate established and his books, which I have examined with admiration and wonder, prove he supplies sermons to preachers of all denominations throughout the United States. This involves a lot of correspondence. Every week he writes a new sermon, prints a large number of copies and sends one to each of his clients. Of course he furnishes but one man in a town or city with his products, but there are a good many towns and cities to supply."

"Is he printing sermons now?" asked Josie.

"Perhaps so; or it may be he is printing some circular to be distributed to the members of the C. I. L. Jim Bennett, the husband of the postmistress here, was once a practical printer, and he is a staunch member of the Irish fraternity. Cragg has known of this underground cavern for years, and at one time it was a regular meeting-place for his order of Champions. So he bought a printing press and, to avoid the prying eyes of his neighbors, established it here. That is the whole story of Cragg's 'crime,' Josie, and it is very simple when once fully explained."

"Do you mean to say you've discovered all this in the two days since you've been here?" asked the girl, in amazement.

"Every bit of it. I came prepared to arrest a gang of counterfeiters, and stumbled on this very interesting but quite harmless plot."

"Where have you been hiding since Sunday?" she inquired.

"Why, I didn't hide at all," he asserted. "Don't you remember giving me a ride yesterday in the Hathaway automobile?"

Josie sat silent. She was glad it was so dark under that shelf of rock, for she would rather her father did not read her humiliation and self-reproach.

"Daddy," she said, with a despairing accent, "I'm going to study to be a cook or a stenographer. I'll never make a decent detective—like Nan, for instance."

O'Gorman laughed.

"Poor Nan!" he exclaimed. "She's been more befuddled than you over this mysterious case. And Cragg is her own father, too. Come, Josie, it's getting late; let's go home."

CHAPTER XXVI

THE PLOT

When they were over the stones and in the lane again, walking arm in arm toward the village, Josie's logical mind turned from her own failure to a consideration of the story her father had just told her.

"I can't understand," she remarked, "how Joselyn came into this affair, what happened to him, or why he is once more the secret associate of old Cragg."

"Joselyn," said the old detective, "is a clever grafter—in other words, an unmitigated scoundrel. Now do you understand?"

"Not quite," confessed Josie.

"He's Irish."

"Isn't his name Scotch?"

"Yes, but Joselyn isn't his name. If you're inclined to pick up his record and follow it through, you'll probably find him pursuing his various adventures under many aliases. He doesn't belong in this country, you know, has only been here

Edith Van Dyne

a few years, so his adventures would probably cover two continents. The fellow always manages to keep just within our laws, although sometimes he gets dangerously near the edge. The world is full of men like Joselyn. They don't interest me."

"Then he belongs to the band of Champions?" asked Josie.

"Yes. In going over Cragg's books and papers in his private office the other night, I found sufficient references to Ned Joselyn to figure out his story with a fair degree of accuracy," said O'Gorman. "He was born in Ireland, got into trouble over there with the authorities, and fled to America, where he met Annabel Kenton and married her. Getting in touch with Old Swallowtail, he joined the Champions and attended to the outside business for Mr. Cragg, purchasing supplies and forwarding them, with money, to the patriots in Ireland. I suppose he made a fair rake-off in all these dealings, but that did not satisfy him. He induced Cragg to invest in some wild-cat schemes, promising him tremendous earnings which could be applied to the Cause. Whether he really invested the money turned over to him, or kept it for himself, is a subject for doubt, but it seems that the old man soon suspected him of double-dealing and they had so many quarrels that Cragg finally threatened to turn him over to the authorities for extradition. That was when our precious Ned thought it wise to disappear, but afterward another peace was patched up, owing largely to the fact that Joselyn knew so much of the workings of the secret order that it was safer to have him for a friend than an enemy."

"I'm thinking of his poor wife," said Josie. "Does she know now where her husband is?"

"I think not. At first, in order to win the confidence of old Cragg, Ned applied considerable of his wife's money to the

Cause, and while she would probably forgive his defalcations he thinks it wiser to keep aloof from her. She foolishly trusted him to 'settle' her mother's estate, and I'm sure he managed to settle most of it on himself. His value to Cragg lay in his ability to visit the different branches of the Champions, which are pretty well scattered throughout the United States, and keep them in touch one with the other. Also he purchased arms and ammunition to be forwarded secretly to Ireland. So you see it was quite impossible for the old man to break with him wholly, rascal though he knows him to be."

"I see," said Josie. "Joselyn has him in his power."

"Entirely so. A hint from him to the authorities would result in an embargo on any further shipments to the rebels in Ireland and so completely ruin the usefulness of the order of Champions. The fellow seems to be a thorn deeply embedded in the side of Old Swallowtail, who will suffer anything to promote the cause of Irish liberty."

"Ingua thinks her grandfather tried to kill Ned, at one time," remarked the girl.

"It's a wonder, with his rabid temper, that he didn't do so," said O'Gorman. "But perhaps he realized that if he was hanged for Joselyn's murder his beloved Order would be without a head and in sorry straits. Thousands of Irishmen are feeding the funds of the Champions, aside from what Cragg himself dumps into the pot. So the old fellow is in a responsible position and mustn't commit murder, however much he may long to, because it would jeopardize the fortunes of his associates. However, the end is not yet, and unless Joselyn acts square in his future dealings he may yet meet with a tragic fate."

Edith Van Dyne

"I wonder what was in that package he took away with him the other night?" mused Josie. "I was sure, at the time, it was counterfeit money."

"It probably contained the monthly printed circular to the various branches of the order. Jim Bennett prints them in that underground cavern and Ned Joselyn sees they are distributed."

"Well," said Josie with a sigh, "you've pricked my bubble, Daddy, and made me ashamed. With all my professed scorn of theories, and my endeavors to avoid them, I walked straight into the theoretic mire and stuck there."

O'Gorman pressed her arm affectionately.

"Never you mind, my dear," in a consoling tone; "you have learned a lesson that will be of great value to you in your future work. I dare not blame you, indeed, for I myself, on the evidence you sent me, came rushing here on a wild-goose chase. One never knows what is on the other side of a page till he turns it, and if we detectives didn't have to turn so many pages, only to find them blank, we'd soon rid the country of its malefactors. But here we are at the Kenton gateway. Go to bed, Josie dear, and pleasant dreams to you."

"Will I see you again?" she asked.

"No; I'm off by the early train. But you must stay here and have your visit out with Mary Louise. It won't hurt you to have a free mind for awhile."

He kissed her tenderly and she went in.

CHAPTER XXVII

NAN'S TRIUMPH

The night's events were not yet ended. An automobile left the edge of the stone-yard, followed a lane and turned into the main highway, where it encountered a woman standing in the middle of the road and waving her arms. She was distinctly visible in the moonlight.

The man with the monocle slowed the car and came to a sudden stop, rather than run her down.

"What's the matter?" he demanded impatiently.

"Wait a minute; I want to talk to you."

"Can't stop," he replied in a querulous tone. "I've got fifty miles to make before daylight. Out of my way, woman."

With a dexterous motion she opened the door and sprang into the seat beside him.

"Here! Get out of this," he cried.

"Drive on," she said calmly. "It'll save time, since you're in a hurry."

Edith Van Dyne

"Get out!"

"I'm going to ride with you. Why bother to argue?"

He turned nervously in his seat to get a look at her, then shifted the clutch and slowly started the car. The woman sat quiet. While bumping over the uneven road at a reckless speed the driver turned at times to cast stealthy glances at the person beside him. Finally he asked in exasperation:

"Do you know where I'm going?"

"You haven't told me."

"Do you know who I am?"

"How should I?"

"Oh, very well," with a sigh of relief. "But isn't this rather—er—irregular?"

"Very."

Again he drove for a time in silence. In the direction they were following they whirled by a village every three or four miles, but the country roads were deserted and the nearest city of any size lay a good fifty miles on.

"I don't know who you are," observed the woman presently, "but I can hazard a guess. You call yourself Joselyn—Ned Joselyn—but that isn't your name. It's the name you married Annabel Kenton under, but it doesn't belong to you."

He gave a roar of anger and started to slow down the car.

"Go ahead!" she said imperatively.

"I won't. You're going to get out of here, and lively, too, or I'll throw you out."

"Do you feel anything against your side?" she asked coolly.

"Yes," with a sudden start.

"It's the muzzle of a revolver. I think it's about opposite your heart and my finger is on the trigger. Go ahead!"

He turned the throttle and the car resumed its former speed.

"Who the deuce are you?" he demanded, in a voice that trembled slightly.

"Like yourself, I have many names," she said. "In Washington they call me Nan Shelley; at Cragg's Crossing I'm Mrs. Scammel, formerly Nan Cragg."

"Oh—ho!" with a low whistle of astonishment. "Nan Cragg, eh! So you've returned from your wanderings, have you?" with a derisive sneer.

"For a time. But in wandering around I've found my place in the world and I'm now a lady detective, not an especially high-class occupation but satisfactory as a bread-winner. I find I'm quite talented; I'm said to be a pretty fair detective."

She could feel him tremble beside her. He moved away from her as far as he could but the pressure against his side followed his movements. After a time he asked defiantly:

"Well, being a detective, what's your business with me? I hope you're not fool enough to think I'm a criminal."

"I don't think it; I know it. You're an unusual sort of a

criminal, too," she replied. "You're mixed up in a somewhat lawless international plot, but it isn't my present business to bring you to book for that."

"What *is* your present business?"

"To discover what you've done with my father's money."

He laughed, as if relieved.

"Spent it for the cause of Ireland."

"Part of it, perhaps. But the bulk of the money you've taken from the Champions of Irish Liberty, most of which came out of my father's own pocket, and practically all the money he gave you to invest for him, you have withheld for your own use."

"You're crazy!"

"I know the bank it's deposited in."

Again he growled, like a beast at bay.

"Whatever I have on deposit is to be applied to the Cause," said he. "It's reserved for future promotion."

"Have you seen to-day's papers?" she inquired.

"No."

"The revolution in Ireland has already broken out."

"Great Scott!" There was sincere anxiety in his voice now.

"It is premature, and will result in the annihilation of all your plans."

"Perhaps not."

"You know better," said she. "Anyhow, your actions are now blocked until we see how the rebellion fares. The Irish will have no further use for American money, I'm positive, so I insist that my father receive back the funds he has advanced you, and especially his own money which he gave you to invest and you never invested."

"Bah! If I offered him the money he wouldn't take it.

"Then I'll take it for him," she asserted. "You'll give up that money because you know I can have you arrested for—well, let us say a breach of American neutrality. You are not a citizen of the United States. You were born in Ireland and have never been naturalized here."

"You seem well posted," he sneered.

"I belong to the Government Secret Service, and the Bureau knows considerable," she replied dryly.

He remained silent for a time, his eyes fixed upon the road ahead. Then he said:

"The Government didn't send you to get Cragg's money away from me. Nor did Cragg send you."

"No, my father is afraid of you. He has been forced to trust you even when he knew you were a treacherous defaulter, because of your threats to betray the Cause. But you've been playing a dangerous game and I believe my father would have killed you, long ago, if—"

Edith Van Dyne

"Well, if what?"

"If you hadn't been his own nephew."

He turned upon her with sudden fierceness.

"Look out!" she called. "I've not the same objection to killing my cousin."

"Your cousin!"

"To be sure. You are the son of Peter Cragg, my father's brother, who returned to Ireland many years ago, when he was a young man. Ned Joselyn is an assumed name; you are Ned Cragg, condemned by the British government for high treason. You are known to be in America, but only I knew where to find you."

"Oh, you knew, did you?"

"Yes; all your various hiding-places are well known to me."

"Confound you!"

"Exactly. You'd like to murder me, Cousin Ned, to stop my mouth, but I'll not give you the chance. And, really, we ought not to kill one another, for the Cragg motto is 'a Cragg for a Cragg.' That has probably influenced my poor father more than anything else in his dealings with you. He knew you are a Cragg."

"Well, if I'm a Cragg, and you're a Cragg, why don't you let me alone?"

"Because the family motto was first ignored by yourself."

For a long time he drove on without another word. Evidently he was in deep thought and the constant pressure of the revolver against his side gave him ample food for reflection. Nan was thinking, too, quietly exulting, the while. As a matter of fact she had hazarded guess after guess, during the interview, only to find she had hit the mark. She knew that Ned Cragg had been condemned by the British government and was supposed to have escaped to America, but not until now was she sure of his identity with Ned Joselyn. Her father had told her much, but not this. Her native shrewdness was alone responsible for the discovery.

"We're almost there, aren't we?" asked Nan at last.

"Where?"

"At the house where you're at present hiding. We've entered the city, I see, and it's almost daybreak."

"Well?"

"I know the Chief of Police here. Am I to have that, money, Cousin Ned, or—"

"Of course," he said hastily.

CHAPTER XXVIII

PLANNING THE FUTURE

It was nearly a month later when Mary Louise, walking down to the river on an afternoon, discovered Ingua sitting on the opposite bank and listlessly throwing pebbles into the stream. She ran across the stepping-stones and joined her little friend.

"How is your grandfather this morning?" she asked.

"I guess he's better," said Ingua. "He don't mumble so much about the Lost Cause or the poor men who died for it in Ireland, but Ma says his broken heart will never mend. He's awful changed, Mary Louise. To-day, when I set beside him, he put out his hand an' stroked my hair an' said: 'poor child— poor child, you've been neglected. After all,' says he, 'one's duties begin at home.' He hasn't had any fits of the devils lately, either. Seems like he's all broke up, you know."

"Can he walk yet?" inquired Mary Louise.

"Yes, he's gett'n' stronger ev'ry day. This mornin' he walked to the bridge an' back, but he was ruther wobbly on his legs. Ma said she wouldn't have left him, just now, if she wasn't sure he'd pick up."

"Oh. Has your mother gone away, then?"

"Left last night," said Ingua, "for Washington."

"Is her vacation over?"

"It isn't that," replied the child. "Ma isn't going to work any more, just now. Says she's goin' to take care o' Gran'dad. She went to Washington because she got a telegram saying that Senator Ingua is dead."

"Senator Ingua?"

"Yes; he was my godfather, you see. I didn't know it myself till Ma told me last night. He was an uncle of Will Scammel, my father that died, but he wasn't very friendly to him an' didn't give him any money while he lived. Ma named me after the Senator, though, 'cause she knew which side her bread was buttered on, an' now he's left me ten thousand dollars in his will."

"Ten thousand!" exclaimed Mary Louise, delightedly, "why, you Craggs are going to be rich, Ingua. What with all the money your mother got back from Ned Joselyn and this legacy, you will never suffer poverty again."

"That's what Ma says," returned the child, simply. "But I dunno whether I'll like all the changes Ma's planned, or not. When she gets back from Washington she's goin' to take me an' Gran'dad away somewheres for the winter, an' I'm to go to a girls' school."

"Oh, that will be nice."

"Will it, Mary Louise? I ain't sure. And while we're gone they're goin' to tear down the old shack an' build a fine new house in its place, an' fix up the grounds so's they're just as good as the Kenton Place."

"Then your mother intends to live here always?"

"Yes. She says a Cragg's place is at Cragg's Crossing, and the fambly's goin' to hold up its head ag'in, an' we're to be some punkins around here. But—I sorter hate to see the old place go, Mary Louise," turning a regretful glance at the ancient cottage from over her shoulder.

"I can understand that, dear," said the other girl, thoughtfully; "but I am sure the change will be for the best. Do you know what has, become of Ned Joselyn?"

"Yes; he an' Annabel Kenton—that's his wife—have gone away somewheres together; somewheres out West, Ma says. He didn't squander Ann's money, it seems; not all of it, anyhow; didn't hev time, I s'pose, he was so busy robbin' Gran'dad. Ned run away from Ann, that time he disappeared, 'cause English spies was on his tracks an' he didn't want to be took pris'ner. That was why he kep' in hidin' an' didn't let Ann know where he was. He was afraid she'd git rattled an' blab."

"Oh; I think I understand. But he will have to keep in hiding always, won't he?"

"I s'pose so. Ma says that'll suit *her,* all right. Am I talkin' more decent than I used to, Mary Louise?"

"You're improving every day, Ingua."

"I'm tryin' to be like you, you know. Ma says I've been a little Arab, but she means to make a lady of me. I hope she will. And then—"

"Well, Ingua?"

"You'll come to visit me, some time, in our new house; won't you?"

"I sure will, dear," promised Mary Louise.

Edith Van Dyne

Other books by this author

Aunt Jane's Nieces

Aunt Jane's Nieces and Uncle John

Aunt Jane's Nieces at Millville

Aunt Jane's Nieces at Work

Aunt Jane's Nieces in Society

Aunt Jane's Nieces in the Red Cross

Aunt Jane's Nieces on Vacation

Aunt Jane's Nieces out West

Mary Louise

Choose from Thousands of 1stWorldLibrary Classics By

A. M. Barnard	Booth Tarkington	Edward Everett Hale
Ada Leverson	Boyd Cable	Edward J. O'Biren
Adolphus William Ward	Bram Stoker	Edward S. Ellis
Aesop	C. Collodi	Edwin L. Arnold
Agatha Christie	C. E. Orr	Eleanor Atkins
Alexander Aaronsohn	C. M. Ingleby	Eleanor Hallowell Abbott
Alexander Kielland	Carolyn Wells	Eliot Gregory
Alexandre Dumas	Catherine Parr Traill	Elizabeth Gaskell
Alfred Gatty	Charles A. Eastman	Elizabeth McCracken
Alfred Ollivant	Charles Amory Beach	Elizabeth Von Arnim
Alice Duer Miller	Charles Dickens	Ellem Key
Alice Turner Curtis	Charles Dudley Warner	Emerson Hough
Alice Dunbar	Charles Farrar Browne	Emilie F. Carlen
Allen Chapman	Charles Ives	Emily Bronte
Alleyne Ireland	Charles Kingsley	Emily Dickinson
Ambrose Bierce	Charles Klein	Enid Bagnold
Amelia E. Barr	Charles Hanson Towne	Enilor Macartney Lane
Amory H. Bradford	Charles Lathrop Pack	Erasmus W. Jones
Andrew Lang	Charles Romyn Dake	Ernie Howard Pie
Andrew McFarland Davis	Charles Whibley	Ethel May Dell
Andy Adams	Charles Willing Beale	Ethel Turner
Angela Brazil	Charlotte M. Braeme	Ethel Watts Mumford
Anna Alice Chapin	Charlotte M. Yonge	Eugene Sue
Anna Sewell	Charlotte Perkins Stetson	Eugenie Foa
Annie Besant	Clair W. Hayes	Eugene Wood
Annie Hamilton Donnell	Clarence Day Jr.	Eustace Hale Ball
Annie Payson Call	Clarence E. Mulford	Evelyn Everett-green
Annie Roe Carr	Clemence Housman	Everard Cotes
Annonaymous	Confucius	F. H. Cheley
Anton Chekhov	Coningsby Dawson	F. J. Cross
Archibald Lee Fletcher	Cornelis DeWitt Wilcox	F. Marion Crawford
Arnold Bennett	Cyril Burleigh	Fannie E. Newberry
Arthur C. Benson	D. H. Lawrence	Federick Austin Ogg
Arthur Conan Doyle	Daniel Defoe	Ferdinand Ossendowski
Arthur M. Winfield	David Garnett	Fergus Hume
Arthur Ransome	Dinah Craik	Florence A. Kilpatrick
Arthur Schnitzler	Don Carlos Janes	Fremont B. Deering
Arthur Train	Donald Keyhoe	Francis Bacon
Atticus	Dorothy Kilner	Francis Darwin
B.H. Baden-Powell	Dougan Clark	Frances Hodgson Burnett
B. M. Bower	Douglas Fairbanks	Frances Parkinson Keyes
B. C. Chatterjee	E. Nesbit	Frank Gee Patchin
Baroness Emmuska Orczy	E. P. Roe	Frank Harris
Baroness Orczy	E. Phillips Oppenheim	Frank Jewett Mather
Basil King	E. S. Brooks	Frank L. Packard
Bayard Taylor	Earl Barnes	Frank V. Webster
Ben Macomber	Edgar Rice Burroughs	Frederic Stewart Isham
Bertha Muzzy Bower	Edith Van Dyne	Frederick Trevor Hill
Bjornstjerne Bjornson	Edith Wharton	Frederick Winslow Taylor

Friedrich Kerst
Friedrich Nietzsche
Fyodor Dostoyevsky
G.A. Henty
G.K. Chesterton
Gabrielle E. Jackson
Garrett P. Serviss
Gaston Leroux
George A. Warren
George Ade
Geroge Bernard Shaw
George Cary Eggleston
George Durston
George Ebers
George Eliot
George Gissing
George MacDonald
George Meredith
George Orwell
George Sylvester Viereck
George Tucker
George W. Cable
George Wharton James
Gertrude Atherton
Gordon Casserly
Grace E. King
Grace Gallatin
Grace Greenwood
Grant Allen
Guillermo A. Sherwell
Gulielma Zollinger
Gustav Flaubert
H. A. Cody
H. B. Irving
H. C. Bailey
H. G. Wells
H. H. Munro
H. Irving Hancock
H. R. Naylor
H. Rider Haggard
H. W. C. Davis
Haldeman Julius
Hall Caine
Hamilton Wright Mabie
Hans Christian Andersen
Harold Avery
Harold McGrath
Harriet Beecher Stowe
Harry Castlemon
Harry Coghill
Harry Houidini

Hayden Carruth
Helent Hunt Jackson
Helen Nicolay
Hendrik Conscience
Hendy David Thoreau
Henri Barbusse
Henrik Ibsen
Henry Adams
Henry Ford
Henry Frost
Henry James
Henry Jones Ford
Henry Seton Merriman
Henry W Longfellow
Herbert A. Giles
Herbert Carter
Herbert N. Casson
Herman Hesse
Hildegard G. Frey
Homer
Honore De Balzac
Horace B. Day
Horace Walpole
Horatio Alger Jr.
Howard Pyle
Howard R. Garis
Hugh Lofting
Hugh Walpole
Humphry Ward
Ian Maclaren
Inez Haynes Gillmore
Irving Bacheller
Isabel Cecilia Williams
Isabel Hornibrook
Israel Abrahams
Ivan Turgenev
J. G.Austin
J. Henri Fabre
J. M. Barrie
J. M. Walsh
J. Macdonald Oxley
J. R. Miller
J. S. Fletcher
J. S. Knowles
J. Storer Clouston
J. W. Duffield
Jack London
Jacob Abbott
James Allen
James Andrews
James Baldwin

James Branch Cabell
James DeMille
James Joyce
James Lane Allen
James Lane Allen
James Oliver Curwood
James Oppenheim
James Otis
James R. Driscoll
Jane Abbott
Jane Austen
Jane L. Stewart
Janet Aldridge
Jens Peter Jacobsen
Jerome K. Jerome
Jessie Graham Flower
John Buchan
John Burroughs
John Cournos
John F. Kennedy
John Gay
John Glasworthy
John Habberton
John Joy Bell
John Kendrick Bangs
John Milton
John Philip Sousa
John Taintor Foote
Jonas Lauritz Idemil Lie
Jonathan Swift
Joseph A. Altsheler
Joseph Carey
Joseph Conrad
Joseph E. Badger Jr
Joseph Hergesheimer
Joseph Jacobs
Jules Vernes
Julian Hawthrone
Julie A Lippmann
Justin Huntly McCarthy
Kakuzo Okakura
Karle Wilson Baker
Kate Chopin
Kenneth Grahame
Kenneth McGaffey
Kate Langley Bosher
Kate Langley Bosher
Katherine Cecil Thurston
Katherine Stokes
L. A. Abbot
L. T. Meade

L. Frank Baum
Latta Griswold
Laura Dent Crane
Laura Lee Hope
Laurence Housman
Lawrence Beasley
Leo Tolstoy
Leonid Andreyev
Lewis Carroll
Lewis Sperry Chafer
Lilian Bell
Lloyd Osbourne
Louis Hughes
Louis Joseph Vance
Louis Tracy
Louisa May Alcott
Lucy Fitch Perkins
Lucy Maud Montgomery
Luther Benson
Lydia Miller Middleton
Lyndon Orr
M. Corvus
M. H. Adams
Margaret E. Sangster
Margret Howth
Margaret Vandercook
Margaret W. Hungerford
Margret Penrose
Maria Edgeworth
Maria Thompson Daviess
Mariano Azuela
Marion Polk Angellotti
Mark Overton
Mark Twain
Mary Austin
Mary Catherine Crowley
Mary Cole
Mary Hastings Bradley
Mary Roberts Rinehart
Mary Rowlandson
M. Wollstonecraft Shelley
Maud Lindsay
Max Beerbohm
Myra Kelly
Nathaniel Hawthrone
Nicolo Machiavelli
O. F. Walton
Oscar Wilde
Owen Johnson
P.G. Wodehouse
Paul and Mabel Thorne

Paul G. Tomlinson
Paul Severing
Percy Brebner
Percy Keese Fitzhugh
Peter B. Kyne
Plato
Quincy Allen
R. Derby Holmes
R. L. Stevenson
R. S. Ball
Rabindranath Tagore
Rahul Alvares
Ralph Bonehill
Ralph Henry Barbour
Ralph Victor
Ralph Waldo Emmerson
Rene Descartes
Ray Cummings
Rex Beach
Rex E. Beach
Richard Harding Davis
Richard Jefferies
Richard Le Gallienne
Robert Barr
Robert Frost
Robert Gordon Anderson
Robert L. Drake
Robert Lansing
Robert Lynd
Robert Michael Ballantyne
Robert W. Chambers
Rosa Nouchette Carey
Rudyard Kipling
Saint Augustine
Samuel B. Allison
Samuel Hopkins Adams
Sarah Bernhardt
Sarah C. Hallowell
Selma Lagerlof
Sherwood Anderson
Sigmund Freud
Standish O'Grady
Stanley Weyman
Stella Benson
Stella M. Francis
Stephen Crane
Stewart Edward White
Stijn Streuvels
Swami Abhedananda
Swami Parmananda
T. S. Ackland

T. S. Arthur
The Princess Der Ling
Thomas A. Janvier
Thomas A Kempis
Thomas Anderton
Thomas Bailey Aldrich
Thomas Bulfinch
Thomas De Quincey
Thomas Dixon
Thomas H. Huxley
Thomas Hardy
Thomas More
Thornton W. Burgess
U. S. Grant
Upton Sinclair
Valentine Williams
Various Authors
Vaughan Kester
Victor Appleton
Victor G. Durham
Victoria Cross
Virginia Woolf
Wadsworth Camp
Walter Camp
Walter Scott
Washington Irving
Wilbur Lawton
Wilkie Collins
Willa Cather
Willard F. Baker
William Dean Howells
William le Queux
W. Makepeace Thackeray
William W. Walter
William Shakespeare
Winston Churchill
Yei Theodora Ozaki
Yogi Ramacharaka
Young E. Allison
Zane Grey